ACCIDENTALLY YOURS

"For My thoughts are not your thoughts, nor are your ways My ways," says the Lord. "For as the heavens are higher than the earth, so are My ways higher than your ways, and My thoughts than your thoughts."

Isaiah 55:8-9 NKJV

Taiwo Iredele Odubiyi

ISBN: 978-978-58630-6-2

Published by:
Tender Heartslink,
Maryland, USA.

Tel.: +1(443)694-6228

Website: www.pastortaiwoodubiyi.org
Facebook: Pastor (Mrs.) Taiwo Odubiyi,
Pastor Taiwo Iredele Odubiyi's Novels & Books,
Twitter: @pastortaiwoodub

Instagram: @pastortaiwoiredeleodubiyi

PRAISES FOR THE BOOKS BY PASTOR TAIWO IREDELE ODUBIYI

I have been reading your books since 2004 during my NYSC days in Kogi State. You are a blessing to Christian homes and this generation. Your fictional stories are God-sent messages to build Christian homes. God shall reward you greatly – *Prince Omoniyi Bamgboye, Ondo State, Nigeria*

Job well done! I started with *Love Fever* in 2011. Ever since, I have read all your books except *Joe and His Step-mother (Bibi)*, which I couldn't get at my regular SU Bookshop in Abeokuta. I have given many people your books as gifts and I have replaced many unreturned copies many times. May the Lord continue to bless and use you for this generation in Jesus' name. You will not be a condemned vessel in Jesus' name - *Pastor Mrs. Ekundayo Adebisi, Abeokuta, Nigeria*

I think I have read one of her books This time around like a million times. It was given to me by Uncle Yinka Odumakin – *Eniolohundasi Enitan Thomas*

Pastor Taiwo Iredele Odubiyi's books have taken me through so many phases in life and it's been a beautiful experience. From the days of singlehood, to my short stint with marriage, to my experience as a young widow. There is always a book for every situation – *pelupelu*

Never Say Never is a book for every man and woman facing one challenge or the other and thinking marriage is not feasible. This book encourages such a person to trust God and believe that there is no challenge bigger than God. What God cannot do does not exist. He will bring a partner that loves you for who you are, no matter the challenge or disability you have. My spirit and soul are blessed by reading this book and I am trusting God more that He will bring me my own partner who will love me and accept me. Beautiful read! I enjoyed reading every line – *Abiodun Ajayi, USA*

Can't wait to get *If You Could See Me Now*. I'm yet to get *Joe and His Stepmother (Bibi)* for my daughter. God will continue to bless you for your lovely and inspiring books. I can confidently tell you that I have all your books – *Mrs. Monisola Alausa, (J.P.) Ayobo, Lagos, Nigeria*

I got your contact from one of your books that I read. I have been blessed, Ma. Thank you for doing what you do. I want to read more of your books and recommend them to my friends - *Oluwatoyin Rose, Akure, Nigeria*

I have always read and enjoyed your books as a single lady and now as a married woman. I just felt that I should contact you and appreciate you for such beautiful novels – *Tabitha, Edo State, Nigeria*

Thank you for making my childhood blissful with your amazing novels – *Omotolani Babalola, Lagos, Nigeria*

Read many of your books- always an eye opener – *tum bamiro*

Tears on My Pillow- very educative. I found myself crying with one of the characters at one point. Will recommend it to everyone (single, dating, married) – *Marian*

I'm one of the readers of your books, even before I got married. I cannot forget *Love Fever*, and others like *Love on the pulpit – Ayobola Babatunde Oloyede*

God will never put His people to shame. Don't believe the report of men but only of God. *Love on the Pulpit* really blessed me – *Janet, USA*

I read *Love on the Pulpit* during my last semester break. This novel is life-changing. Thank you for giving hope to the hopeless, and the understanding that in God, all things are possible. I just got two of your novels. Can't wait to be done with my exams so I can read them – *Princess Amaka*

Currently reading the book *Never Say Never.* Thank you for being a blessing – *Ibrahim Olabisi*

I read one of your books *Is it me you're looking for*, it is so interesting and taught me many lessons I can never forget – *Abiodun Agboola*

If You Could See Me Now- I read it. Awesome! – *Toyin Olatunji*

EXCERPTS

… John waited for Lola to end the call, and then he put the phone down. He was lying on his back, in bed, and as he stared at the ceiling, thinking of her, his heart seemed to ache with what he had not said. After some minutes, he took his phone and sent a message to her.

Lola, I'm falling in love with you.

****

Lola's phone alerted her of a message and she took the phone. When she saw his name, she tapped on it to read, and what she saw made her smile broadly. …

… John got down from his car, and with a smile in place, he waited for Lola.

****

As Lola went outside to meet John, her heart was doing somersaults. She opened the gate of the house, stepped out, and saw him standing beside his car. …

… They did not talk for some seconds, and then he said, "I always smile when I remember how we met."

"Me too. I almost did not attend the event, you know." She smiled and looked down.

"I almost did not attend too because of my arm. I came only because I did not want to disappoint Dayo. He wanted to hook me up with Mercy's friend, Lekan."

Surprise jerked her head up. "To meet Lekan?" …

ACKNOWLEDGMENTS

I thank You, Lord God, the I AM, my Rescuer and Lord, For:

Yet another book. Thank You for the great privilege and grace that You have given me to speak and write for You, and about You: about Your will, Your ways, Your word, and Your wondrous love. Thank You for the mercy You have shown me to know You;

My husband, Rev. Sola Odubiyi, and my children—for all that they do for me.

The wonderful family members You have blessed me with—for their always being there for me.

Babatope Olabode—my editor. *Thank you for choosing to work with me. With keen eyes and skill, you made this book better. I appreciate you.*

Families, friends, and fans (my avid readers)—those who have been with me since the beginning of this great journey, and those who joined along the way, reading my books, supporting, praying, and encouraging me.

Lord, I wouldn't have been able to accomplish much without these amazing people You have brought my way. I am grateful. Let those who read each of these books be blessed, touched and transformed by You, that they may know that You are the real Author and Your mercy endures forever!

It's All About You! **Taiwo Iredele Odubiyi**

DEDICATION

To God

To every man who is the husband of a female pastor;
who does not feel threatened by his wife's calling,
but supports her with his own divine calling.

To every woman who is called to pastor.

****

To:

Pastor's husband and his wife.

Don't let anyone think less of you because of your calling.

I pray you will be a good example to all believers in what you say, in the way you live, in your love, your faith, your purity, and your support of your spouse's divine calling, in Jesus' name.

1 Timothy 4:12

Dear reader, thank you for choosing this book. I hope you enjoy reading it as much as I did, writing it.

You will reunite with some characters in *The Forever Kind of Love* and *If You Could See Me Now*

Take the stage Lord.
And have Your way
I'm just a vessel.
And nothing more
And when You're done
Please take the glory.
I'm satisfied, just to see You glorified

- Nathaniel Bassey

CHAPTER 1

As Lola began to eat the second piece of fish on her plate, she drew her phone which was on the table closer, went on YouTube, and searched for the video of Kathryn Kuhlman which she was watching last night. She found it and pressed play.

"I believe in miracles!" The female American evangelist began, in the video.

The time was eight-thirty five on that Monday evening, December 30, and twenty-nine-year-old Lola Thomas who returned home from work about half an hour ago, was alone at the dining table, eating fried rice and fish. The dining area was on a side of the moderately furnished living room of the three-bedroom bungalow which she lived in with her mother and grandparents.

Lola was tall, slim, and slightly light-skinned, like her mother, Seun Alabi.

Seun Alabi, an actress, was seated in the living room, watching a show on TV. Lola's grandmother, called *Grandma* by everyone including her children, had gone to the house of one of her daughters since Thursday and would return on New Year Day. Lola's grandfather,

Grandpa, had complained of feverish feeling and gone to bed early.

"Because I believe in God!" Kathryn Kuhlman went on.

Just then, Lola's phone started to ring, thereby pausing the video on YouTube. The phone screen revealed that the call was from one of her many cousins, Mercy, and she accepted the call.

"Mercy, how are you?" Lola greeted the younger lady.

"I'm doing well, thank you." Mercy answered. "And you?"

"I'm fine, thank you." Lola continued eating as she talked with Mercy.

"And thanks for your call yesterday. I appreciate it." Mercy said.

Yesterday was Mercy's twenty fourth birthday, and Lola had called to wish her a happy birthday.

"You're welcome." Lola responded. "Hope you enjoyed your day."

"I sure did." Mercy said and giggled.

"Great!"

"Er… just a quick one, Lola," Mercy began to tell her why she'd really called, "A friend, Dayo, is having a get-together for his friends on Wednesday, first of January. He and his friends are good Christians. I'm going to be there, and I've invited my friend, Lekan, to come along." (Read ***The Forever Kind of Love***)

Lola knew Lekan to be Mercy's very close friend. She had met Lekan a couple of times and had her phone number.

"I'm inviting you to the event as well." She heard Mercy say.

"A get-together by your friend, Dayo?"

"Yes," Mercy responded.

"For his friends?!" Lola repeated with a frown as she wondered, *what has that got to do with me? Why do I have to attend?*

"Yes. They are sound Christians." Mercy said.

"You know that they are sound Christians because?"

"Because I've known Dayo for some time and I know that he's a solid Christian. I've met some of his friends and I know that they are solid Christians too. They meet regularly for prayer, and er… Dayo is my fiancé."

"Your fiancé?" When Lola said that, she saw her mother glance at her.

"Yes." Mercy confirmed.

Lola looked away from her mother as she told Mercy, "Oh, I didn't know that."

"He actually proposed to me today." Mercy revealed to her.

"Oh, wow! That's great! Congrats." Lola could see from the corner of her eyes that her mother was still looking at her, obviously listening to her side of the conversation.

"Thank you." Mercy responded.

"So, you were talking about the get-together," Lola said, bringing them back to the reason for the call.

"Yes. When Dayo mentioned the get-together, I told him that I'd want to invite you and Lekan to it, and he said it's fine."

As Lola listened to Mercy, her eyes bounced around the living room which had large windows, a gray sofa, two armchairs, a loveseat, and six small corner tables. The room with gray and black rug also had a large flat screen TV, two console tables, a large mirror on a side, and artworks on its cream-colored walls.

"What's the get-together about? Is it to celebrate your relationship, his birthday, or something else?" Lola asked.

"No. He and his friends meet regularly for fellowship and it's his turn to host them." Mercy explained.

"I don't get it," Lola said, "He's hosting his friends and you want me to be there?!"

"Yes. I'm inviting you and Lekan because some of the men that will be there are very much single."

Lola snorted and rolled her eyes even though Mercy could not see her. "Where will it hold?"

"In his apartment which he has just rented."

Lola laughed a little and said, "Er- I'm not sure I want to come. Thanks for having me in mind though. I appreciate it."

"No, please come." Mercy insisted.

"I can't attend!" Lola said and pushed her empty plate away from her.

"Why not?"

Lola chuckled and said, "One, the people are your friends, not mine. I don't know them. And two, it's in Dayo's house. I don't know about Lekan, but it would be awkward for me. It's not my kind of thing."

"It doesn't matter, Lola."

"It does matter! I'm being invited simply because some single Christian men will be there. What does that make me- a desperate spinster? No, no. I want to get married, but I'm not desperate. Besides, I won't know anyone there."

"You don't need to know them. Don't forget that you're not going to be alone; I will be there, and Lekan will be there—"

"So, Lekan doesn't mind attending?"

"No, she doesn't." Mercy answered.

Lekan may not mind, but I do mind. I'm a Pastor in my church and I need to be careful, Lola thought.

Mercy added, "Some ladies will also be there and all of them are Christians. If I didn't think it's okay, I wouldn't invite you- I wouldn't even be there myself."

"Mercy, I don't know—"

"You and Lekan can come together,

"Lekan is not even my friend, she's your friend."

"Yes, but she's not a stranger to you. You can sit together and leave whenever you want."

Lola did not talk for some seconds as she considered the proposal and checked her spirit.

"Did you say Wednesday?" She asked, to confirm.

"Yes."

That's in two days' time. "What time?"

"At four in the afternoon." Mercy answered.

Lola would be going to church in the morning on that New Year Day and would be back at home, latest one in the afternoon. She did not think she had anything planned for the rest of the day. *Hmm. To go, or not to go*?

"What time will you get there?" She asked Mercy.

"I will be going there much earlier, to meet his family."

"They will be there?"

"Yes." Mercy answered. "So, you see, it's okay, it's safe. I want you to come."

"What about Lekan? When does she plan to get there?" Lola wanted to know.

"We haven't discussed that, but I guess she will be there around four when the event will start." Mercy responded.

Lola carried her glass cup of water, drank a little water, and as she put the cup down, she asked, "Where does she live?"

Mercy told her.

"And where is Dayo's house?"

Mercy answered.

Lola took a deep breath, and then said, "Well, two things—one, I'll say now that I'll come, but if I feel different about it later, I'll let you know, which means that I won't attend."

Mercy agreed.

"Two, if Lekan will attend, I'll pick her up." She decided. She'd prefer to go in her car so she could leave whenever she wanted. She wouldn't want to be delayed unnecessarily or get stranded.

"Okay, good." Mercy agreed.

"Well, tell Lekan to expect me anytime from three in the afternoon."

"Alright, thanks."

"But as I've said," Lola quickly added, "I will pray, and it's possible I change my mind."

"I understand, and I will pray that you don't change your mind."

"Whatever,"

They laughed.

Lola spoke again, "You can send both Dayo's and Lekan's addresses to me."

"Okay, I will. How's Mommy?"

Lola's mother and Mercy's mother were sisters, although Mercy's mother was late.

"She's doing well, thank you." Lola answered.

"Extend my greetings to her."

"I will. And how's everyone over there?" Lola asked. "Your siblings, Stella, Papa, everyone?"

Papa was Mr. Alabi, their uncle, and Mercy and her three siblings lived with his family. Papa, a retired police officer was the first of Grandpa and Grandma's five children, and the only male. He was nicknamed Papa by his nieces and nephews because he played the role of a big brother to his four younger sisters. Mercy's mother was his immediate younger sister, followed by Seun Alabi, and then two younger sisters. When Mercy's mother died ten years ago, Papa brought Mercy and her siblings into his house and took care of them along with his own five children. His second child, Stella, an Accountant, was a year older than Mercy and very close to Mercy.

"Everyone is fine, thank you." Mercy responded.

Mercy and Lola chatted for about a minute more and then said goodnight.

The moment the call ended, Seun Alabi asked her daughter, "Was that Mercy?"

Lola had known that her mother would ask questions. "Yes, and she asked after you."

"Alright. Is she doing well?"

"Yes."

"Did she say that a man proposed to her?" Seun Alabi asked.

"Yes—today."

"Today? That's good." Seun Alabi said. "So, what are they celebrating?"

"It's not really a celebration. She said that the man is having a get-together for his friends, and she wants me to attend." Lola explained to her mother.

Seun Alabi did not talk, and Lola did not talk.

Lola knew that her mother would be thinking about her and would most likely be praying for her under her breath now because Lola who was her only child, an ordained pastor, and five years older than Mercy, was still very much single. Lola was supposed to marry four years ago, but the man died.

Knowing that her mother might ask further questions about Mercy and her fiancé, which she didn't think she would like to answer, Lola got up, took her empty plate and used utensils, and went to the kitchen.

She washed them and when she returned to the living room, she asked her mother if they could pray now, as the family prayed together every night. Her mother said yes, and they prayed for about fifteen minutes, committing the family, the night, and the New Year, into God's hands.

When Lola stood immediately after the prayer, her mother asked if she was going into her room to sleep.

"Yes, although I'm not sleeping right away. There's a video I'm watching on YouTube."

Her mother opened her mouth to talk, but changed her mind, and closed it. Then taking a deep breath, she exhaled it, and said, "Okay, goodnight, God bless you."

"Amen. Goodnight, Mom." Lola responded and went in the direction of her bedroom. The medium size room with two windows and a brown rug, had a twin bed, closet, a mirror that hung on the back of the room door, a ceiling fan, a six-drawer dresser which also served as her bedside table, and chair, among other things.

Turning on the room light and fan, she sat on her bed, put her phone down beside her, and stared blankly at the wall as she began to think about her life.

Her mother, Seun Alabi, was a teenager, and in the final year of High School when she conceived her. Seun Alabi had been impregnated by her Social Studies teacher. The twenty-six-year-old man who was planning his wedding at the time was also the coordinator of the school's drama group of which Seun was an active member. When the atrocity became known, the school's management suspended the man while Seun stayed away from school. The man did not want to have anything to do with the pregnant girl however, and she and the baby in her womb became the responsibility of her parents.

Seun was sixteen when she gave birth to Lola and shortly after, she returned to school. She eventually graduated from High School and went on to study Theater Arts in University. Following her passion, Seun Alabi soon became a known face in secular movies and had a male child for a movie producer, but the child died at eight months old.

Lola who was raised by her grandparents was seventeen and in the first year of university when she became a Christian. The following year, her father, Bade Thomas, now a Professor of Sociology, contacted them and asked to be a part of Lola's life. They later discovered that he did not have a child with his wife.

Lola's mother, now forty five years old, also became a Christian at about the time that her immediate older sister, Mercy's mother, died which was ten years ago. Open about her faith, Seun Alabi switched over from acting in secular movies to Christian movies.

Lola and Seun Alabi continued living with Lola's grandparents in their rented apartment while Seun Alabi began to build her house. Lola graduated from the University and when she began to work in a bank, she supported her mother financially, and soon, the three-bedroom bungalow with a large compound was completed. Mother and daughter moved into it with Lola's grandparents, six years ago, and Seun Alabi employed a domestic worker, Anna, to help around the house. The middle-aged woman who was a Christian, came to the house at six in the morning, and closed at four in the evening, Monday to Saturday.

Because Seun Alabi did not marry, she prayed for Lola everyday to get married and have children on time. This sometimes made Lola feel under pressure- at such times however, she talked to God and reminded Him of His promises to her.

Lola would like to be married and she had come across some men, but she had not met the right man. Shortly after the death of her fiancé, Chege, a married deacon in the church she attended and where Chege was a pastor until his death, wanted to befriend her. Upset, Lola told her mother, and her family decided to leave the church and join *Word of God Church*. Some eligible men were in *Word of God Church* and she was friends with most of them, but none of them had shown interest in her. A man at her workplace would like to marry her but he was not a serious Christian. And so, Lola was still praying and trusting God to be married.

Lola's mind returned to Mercy's phone call. Mercy had said that Dayo proposed to her today, and this made Lola remember how Chege proposed to her.

Inhaling deeply, her mind went to the past. She was twenty four while Chege, a Kenyan, was five years older than her when they began their relationship. The architect was a pastor in the church that they both attended and when he showed interest in her, she was elated. She had been hoping and praying to marry a pastor since she discovered that her divine purpose was to be a pastor, and now Pastor Chege had shown up.

A month into the relationship however, he began to ask her for sex, to her surprise. She had been keeping herself; she would not want to sin against God, and she told Chege so, but he said that God would forgive them if they sinned. No one was perfect, he was quick to add. And that was how Lola found herself regularly asking God for forgiveness for the sin she was about to commit with Pastor Chege.

She knew that they were wrong, but it seemed easier for her to compromise and please Pastor Chege, than to stand for God.

At a time, her conscience could no longer tolerate the sinful life and it crossed her mind a number of times to expose this sin to the senior pastor of the church so that they could be helped but she did not, for two reasons. One, Chege would not want her to take that step as he was well liked and respected in the church. He was a fiery preacher and he loved to preach. He would definitely be suspended by the pastor if his sin was exposed, and Lola did not want that to happen to him. Two, she was sure that he was going to marry her. If they got married, having sex would no longer be sinful, and everything would be alright.

And so, nobody knew what was going on, not even her mother or very close friend, Sarah.

Lola and Chege were in a relationship for a year and hoped to be married the following year when he died, shattering their plans. She almost couldn't believe that everything had ended abruptly.

As she mourned his death and the death of her wedding plans, she couldn't help wondering—was it satan who took him out, or did God remove him from the stage? Did his death just happen, or was it a consequence of his sinful lifestyle? Some pastors knew and feared God, but it became clear to Lola now that Chege was not one of them. He belonged to the group of pastors that dragged the name of God in the mud through sinful and evil practices.

Realizing that she had become confused and gone into a spiritual slumber while in the relationship with Chege, she rededicated herself to God, asked God to have mercy on her, and renew a right spirit in her. One of the songs she found herself singing at that time was – *Take me back, take me back, dear Lord, to the place where I first received You – by Andrae Crouch.*

Chege's death had hit Lola's mother almost as much as it hit Lola because Lola's mother liked him. She had accepted him as the son she never had and was already looking forward to her daughter's wedding to the dynamic pastor, unaware of what Chege had been doing behind closed doors. That was four years ago.

...Lola wrenched her mind back to the present. She was happy for Mercy as she and her three siblings had gone through a lot. Mercy was the oldest of four children, and fourteen years old when their mother died. Their father had left them before their mother died, to start a family with another woman, and when their mother died ten years ago at the age of thirty seven, their uncle, *Papa*, took them in. The time that Mercy's mother died was a tough time for everyone concerned, especially Grandpa and Grandma who had lost an adult child, their first daughter.

Lola would have loved to call her friend, Sarah, and tell her about Mercy's invitation to the get-together, but Sarah got married just on Saturday, and was on honeymoon with her husband. If Sarah had not been married, she would have invited her along. Sarah had not contacted her since Saturday, and she did not think she should contact her at this time of the night.

Hmm, it is well, Lola said under her breath, and then decided to pray about the get-together. Closing her eyes, she told God, "Let me know if I should go or not, counsel me in Jesus' name."

Afterward, she stood to change into her sleepwear. The clothes she wore to the bank where she worked were on the chair and she took them to hang in her closet. She wore her sleepwear, got in bed, and took her phone.

CHAPTER 2

That Monday evening at about nine-forty five, John was in his official car, on his way home from visiting a friend, when he received a call from another friend and a church member, Dayo. Dayo had called him last night to invite him to a get-together in his apartment on Wednesday, January 1. He had accepted the invitation, and he guessed that this call from Dayo was to give him further information about it.

After the greetings, Dayo asked him, “Are you still coming to my house on Wednesday?”

“Yes, I’ll be there by God’s grace.”

“Good. There's someone I'll introduce to you.”

“Who is the person? A male or a female?”

“A female.”

John laughed. “Why? Who is she?”

“She's Mercy's very good friend.”

John had not met Mercy, but Dayo had been telling him about her.

“And so?”

“You can become friends too.” Dayo said.

They laughed and John told him, “You're not serious.”

"It's just for you to meet her."

"When did you become a matchmaker, Dayo?" John asked, amusement obvious in his voice.

"I'm not matchmaking. I will only introduce you. That's all."

"You don't have to, I can get my own wife, thank you." He said.

"Sure, I know that. We're not forcing anything… but who knows?"

John laughed again. "Okay, we'll see how it goes."

"Alright, I'll talk to you later."

After the call, John thought about what Dayo said and chuckled. He had been in a relationship but it did not work out. He would turn thirty one in August and he guessed that Dayo was doing this because he had told Dayo sometime ago that he hoped he'd meet the right woman and be married in the new year.

John worked in Akure, Ondo state, Nigeria, in the regional office of *Intent Home,* a company that sold home and wall décor. He graduated seven years ago from the University where he studied Business Administration. He could not get a job for about a year however, and as such, when *Intent Home* offered him a job in the regional office, he gladly accepted it even though the salary was not much. He accepted for four reasons: the salary was better than nothing, it came with an official car and accommodation which he would share with another staff, and he believed that being in a regional office would give him an opportunity to progress within the company. He moved to Akure and only visited his family in Lagos once in about two months.

But now, even though he knew that being in a regional office had benefits, he didn't think that he was making much progress in that company, and he had decided to get another job which was why he had gone out to see his friend.

He arrived Lagos on December 20 for Christmas holiday, and would be around till fourth of January when he would travel back to Akure.

Soon, he got home, a one-story building owned by his parents, drove inside the compound, and parked his car. His parents and younger brother, Matthew, lived in the front apartment while the back apartment and the two upstairs were rented out. His older brother was married and had relocated to Germany with his family last year. There were four bedrooms in the apartment, and John still had his room which he stayed in whenever he came home from Akure.

Alighting from the car, he locked up the doors, entered the apartment, and saw his parents in the living room, with Matthew, Matthew's friend and the friend's fiancé. He greeted them and when his mother told him that food was on the dining table, he got it, brought it to the living room, and lowered himself into one of the comfortable leather chairs.

Seeing Matthew's friend and his fiancé made John remember what Dayo had told him. *Should I meet this lady*?

Can I trust Dayo's judgment? He thought about Dayo-he was a serious-minded Christian like him. They met in *Great Grace Chapel* and became good friends. John used to attend *Cornerstone Church* with his parents and brothers, but when he went to university in another town, he attended

Great Grace Chapel Campus Fellowship, and that was how he became a member of the church.

When John finished eating, he took his tray to the kitchen and washed the used items, before heading to his room. Turning on the light and ceiling fan in the room, he walked up to his bedside table and put his car keys and phone on top of a sheet of paper on the table, to prevent the paper from being blown away by the fan.

The paper was a list of the four things he would want God to do for him in the new year: a better job, an additional stream of income, establishment of his ministry, and marriage. The pastor of *Great Grace Chapel,* the church he attended in Lagos, had told the members to trust God for additional streams of income in the new year.

John bent down and pulled out from under his bed a bag that contained his clothes that he did not want again. In church yesterday, it was announced that the church would be reaching out to the less privileged in the neighborhood on the first Sunday of the new year, and church members were asked to donate wearable clothes and shoes.

Opening the box, he brought out the clothes and checked them to be sure that they were in good condition, and afterward, he folded them neatly and put them in a big plastic bag. He decided to take them to *Great Grace Chapel* tomorrow morning as he would not be in the church in the evening for New Year cross-over night service. He had promised to go with his family to their own church for the cross-over night service, and he would be traveling back to Akure on Saturday morning.

****

"And you know before I ever said it… I believe in miracles, and that is happening today. As long as God still answers prayers… there will always be miracles. Remember that… you and I believe in miracles because we believe in God, and in the power of prayer." Kathryn Kuhlman said in the video that Lola had been watching on YouTube.

Lola's phone alerted her of a WhatsApp chat, and she paused the video to check the chat.

Hi, how are you? This is Lekan. All the best in the New Year in Jesus' name.

Lekan? Good, I'll like to talk with her. Smiling, Lola responded immediately.

Amen. A happy New Year in advance in Jesus' name. Has Mercy discussed with you?

While she waited for Lekan's reply, she checked chats on WhatsApp, and that was when she remembered that a member of her High School group was celebrating her birthday that day. Opening the group chat, she posted a prayer.

The Lord bless you and protect you. The Lord smile on you and be gracious to you. The Lord show you His favor and give you His peace, in Jesus' name. (Numbers 6:24-26 NLT) Happy Birthday.

When she saw Lekan's response drop on her phone, she closed the group chat and opened Lekan's chat.

Yes. Are you free to talk?

Lola typed her response.

Sure.

Almost immediately, her phone began to ring, and she answered it.

She and Lekan exchanged pleasantries and then began to discuss the invitation to the get-together.

Lola repeated what she had told Mercy and added, "It will be awkward for me. The people coming for the event are Dayo's friends. We'll probably be the only ones who are not, and we have been invited only to meet his unattached male friends. That doesn't sound good."

"Funny enough, I don't mind." Lekan said and giggled. "They are Christians. I've met Dayo and some of his friends, so I don't mind attending. As a matter of fact, I brought up the idea. I met Dayo and some of his friends yesterday evening at the dinner in celebration of his and Mercy's birthday—"

"Did you say, 'his and Mercy's birthday'?"

Lekan giggled. "Yes, both of them are the same day, December 29,"

"That's interesting." Lola commented.

Lekan went on, "When I saw that they are committed Christians, I told Mercy to ask Dayo if he has friends who are available."

"You said that just yesterday, and now he's inviting us to an event. Doesn't that look somehow?"

"As I've said, I've met Dayo and some of those people. They are responsible Christians. If God wants us to meet a man there, fine. If not, it's fine too. Let's just pray about it and attend." Lekan said with enthusiasm. "We will sit together and leave when we want. Don't forget that Mercy is going to be there as well, and she said that Dayo's parents will be there."

When Lola still hesitated, Lekan added, "Let's attend, don't forget the saying- *nothing ventured, nothing gained.* See it as an opportunity to meet some Christians and have a good time on New Year Day. It will be better than being at home eating popcorn with only the TV for company."

"Popcorn and TV," Lola said and chuckled. She had eaten popcorn while watching TV many times; the two combine well.

"Yes, think about it."

Lekan had a point—it would be an opportunity to meet people, Lola thought. *I've prayed about it and if I sense anything in my spirit before the day, I'll pull back.*

"Okay." She agreed.

They decided on the time that Lola would pick her up and then said goodnight.

Lola glanced at the time; it was now ten-forty five. Closing YouTube, she went online to search for a post: *Excerpts from the book—Daughter of Destiny by Jamie Buckingham.*

She had this book, which was about Kathryn Kuhlman, as well as Roberts Liardon's book titled *God's Generals:*

Why They Succeeded and Why Some Failed, that featured Kathryn Kuhlman.

She had been posting portions of the excerpts from the book on Facebook for about two weeks, with the hope that her Facebook friends would learn some important lessons from the life of the female American evangelist.

Lola found the excerpts, copied the part that she would like to post tomorrow morning, and pasted it in a note on her phone, to save it. Afterward, she prayed, and slept.

Her alarm woke her up at five-thirty on Tuesday morning, and she got up to prepare for work. At five-fifty eight, the housekeeper called her phone to let her know that she had arrived, and Lola went outside to open the gate for her.

Back in her room, she took her phone and posted the excerpts about Kathryn Kuhlman on Facebook.

When she was all set, she walked toward her mother's room and opened the door. Seun Alabi was in bed, still sleeping.

"Good morning, Mommy." She called out.

Her mother stirred and woke up.

"I'm leaving for work."

"Okay, good morning, and God bless you."

"Amen." Lola responded.

She checked on her grandfather too. "How do you feel today?"

He said that he felt better, and she prayed for him briefly.

When she was ready to leave, the housekeeper followed her to open and close the gate.

Entering her car, Lola drove out of the compound and headed for *Dominion Bank Limited* where she had been working for about seven years.

As she drove on, she thought about the get-together. Aside working in a bank and being a pastor, she was twenty nine years old and would probably be older than Dayo and his friends. Why should she attend?

Different excuses occurred to her, but somehow, she sensed in her spirit that she should keep an open mind about it and attend.

Hmm, okay, I'll attend it, she decided.

Being the last day of the year, the bank closed early at two in the afternoon, to reopen on Thursday, second of January. She went home and there, her grandfather was in the living room with her mother, and she greeted them. The housekeeper who opened the gate for her went to the kitchen to continue her work.

Lola looked at her grandfather. The man who would turn eighty in January, was drinking pap, a Nigerian meal made from fermented corn. In a flat plate on the table in front of him was *moinmoin*, a Nigerian steamed bean pudding, and beside him was his walking stick.

"How do you feel, Grandpa?"

"I'm much better, thank you."

"I'm glad to hear that." She said.

"He looks better." Her mother added.

Lola agreed. "He definitely does. Praise God!"

"What time are we leaving for the New Year's Eve cross-over night service?" Grandpa asked.

"We'll need to leave around eight-thirty." Lola answered. "Will you be able to go to church with us?"

"Yes."

Lola looked at her mother.

Her mother shrugged. "He can go."

"Okay. Is there something to eat, Mom?"

"Yes, it's in the kitchen."

"Thanks, Mom."

Lola went to her room to change her clothes, and after eating, she returned to her room to rest.

While in her room, her friend, Sarah, called her. Lola and Sarah had been friends since her second year in university. They attended the same campus fellowship and later became roommates. Sarah who majored in journalism and had a master's degree, worked for a major newspaper, and had a weekly column.

"So good to hear your voice." Lola said excitedly. "How are you and your hubby?"

"We're enjoying ourselves." Sarah said and laughed.

"I'm sure you are,"

They giggled.

"Are you back at home?"

"Yes." Lola answered.

Sarah appreciated Lola for her gift, support, prayers, and all that Lola did for her wedding. "My husband and I are so grateful,"

"*My husband and I*! Wow!"

They laughed.

"Thanks for being there for us." Sarah added.

"The pleasure was mine. What are we friends for?" Lola responded.

She asked if Sarah had seen the wedding pictures she sent to her on WhatsApp, and Sarah said no.

"My husband and I agreed to stay away from social media this one week as much as possible, so I have not checked my WhatsApp chats." Sarah explained. "I'll check them after the call. So, how have you been?"

Lola answered that she was doing well, and then she told her friend about the get-together, and that she had decided to attend.

"Okay, keep me informed." Sarah said and added that she and her husband would return from their honeymoon on Sunday.

After the call, Lola slept, and when she came out of her room around five-forty, the housekeeper had left. At about eight-thirty in the evening, they all went to church for the cross-over service.

****

In the morning of that Tuesday, John went to *Great Grace Chapel* to donate the clothes. Dropping the bag of clothes in the secured container that had been provided by the church for donation of clothes and shoes, he returned to his car, and left.

Just as he was packing his car at home, his mother called his phone and asked him to help her buy a crate of eggs from a nearby store. He got down from the car, locked up, and walked out of the compound to go to the store.

On the way, he received a call from a childhood friend who had relocated to London and while he talked on the phone, he tripped on a cracked concrete on a sidewalk, and fell.

The people around came close. "Are you okay?"

"Yes, I guess." He answered as he picked himself up.

A lady picked up his scattered phone and gave it to him.

"Thank you."

He checked himself—his shirt and trousers were dirty, and there was blood on his right arm. He could not continue to the store in the state he was in, and he returned home.

When his mother saw him, she felt very bad and responsible for what happened to him. His father drove him to a clinic where the arm was treated and bandaged, and back at home, he ate, took the medication he was given, and went to sleep.

He woke up around four-thirty in the afternoon, and when he saw a missed call from Matthew, he returned the call. Apparently, their mother had informed Matthew of John's accident, and Matthew wanted to know how his brother was feeling.

After the call, John went to the kitchen, to look for something to eat. Opening the refrigerator, he put some sliced fruits on a ceramic plate, took a fork, and returned to his bedroom.

When Matthew returned home in the evening at about six, he came to John's room, and sat down. While chatting, John told him that Dayo had invited him to his house the next day for a get-together, and he would need a ride.

Matthew knew Dayo and he said, "No problem, but must you attend? Why don't you stay at home and rest, more so, as tomorrow is New Year Day."

"I've promised Dayo that I'll be there." John responded and looked down at his bandaged arm. "I'm fine, I'll attend it."

"What's the get-together for?"

"He said that it's just to come together with some of his friends and celebrate the New Year." John explained, and when he remembered what Dayo told him last night, he smiled and added, "He also wants me to meet a lady."

"A lady? Why?"

John laughed. "He said that she's his fiancé's friend."

"Is that why you want to attend the event, to meet the lady?"

John shook his head. "No, no."

Matthew shrugged and stood. "Will you still be able to go to church with us this evening?"

"Sure." John answered. "Er—do you think you'll be able to drive me down to Akure on Saturday? If it's not convenient, I can talk to a friend."

Matthew agreed to drive him to Akure and board a bus back to Lagos.

At nine-thirty that evening, John went with his family to *Cornerstone Church* for the Watchnight service, and when it was time to testify of the Lord's goodness in the year, his mother was among those who went out. Soon, it was her turn, and she mentioned some of the things that God did in her life and family in the year.

She went on, "And this morning, one of my sons had an accident, tripping on a cracked concrete on a sidewalk. I'm so glad that it was not serious, it could have been worse, and I give God all the glory."

The service was eventually brought to a close around twelve-forty five in the morning, and they returned home. His parents went straight into their bedroom to sleep, while Matthew opened the refrigerator to get food to eat. He invited John to join him, but John declined and explained that he would be fasting that day. He fasted every first day of the month and every Monday.

"You will be fasting on New Year Day?" Matthew asked.

"Why not?"

Matthew chuckled. "I also fast on the first day of every month, but today's special."

"That's all the more reason I need to observe the fasting - today's special."

"You're right." Matthew admitted. "Well, I didn't plan to fast today, so I'll do it tomorrow."

John shrugged.

"Lord, forgive me." Matthew said under his breath.

John laughed and went to his room. Before he slept, he forwarded new year prayers to some of his phone contacts. Afterward, he thanked God again for bringing every member of his family into the new year and thanked Him in advance for answers to his four prayer requests.

****

The cross-over service in the church where Lola and her family worshipped, *Word of God Church*, ended around one in the morning and Lola returned home with her mother and grandfather.

At nine-thirty in the morning, Lola and her mother were back in church for New Year Day service which began at ten and lasted about an hour and a half.

Back at home, Lola made two posts on Facebook- one was a continuation of Kathryn Kuhlman's story, and the other was a prayer for the New Year. Afterward, she joined her mother in the kitchen to get lunch ready while Grandpa was in the living room. The housekeeper, Anna, had been given the day off. As mother and daughter cooked, they talked and laughed. Seun Alabi asked after Sarah, and Lola answered that she called Sarah earlier in the day.

They were about to eat lunch when Seun Alabi received a call from her immediate younger sister. The woman wanted Seun Alabi to know that she would reach her house in about four minutes, and that she would need Lola's assistance to carry Grandma's bags. Seun Alabi related the message to Lola, and Lola got up, wore her slippers, and went outside.

When they arrived, Lola opened the gate so her aunt could bring her car inside the compound. Lola greeted them, wished them a happy New Year, and carried her grandmother's three bags.

Inside the house, they all gathered around the lunch table and talked as they ate.

They began to discuss Grandpa's eightieth birthday that would be coming up on January 18. Grandpa had told them in November when his birthday was brought up that he would not want a party as he would like to honor the memory of his daughter. It would be ten years since his first daughter—Mercy's mother—passed away on December 26 and the family intended to have special prayer on that day for her children and the entire family.

And now, the women at the lunch table began to make arrangements about a birthday cake, and food and drinks for the family members that would definitely come on Grandpa's birthday as it fell on a Saturday.

"It would be nice to inform our pastor so he can come and pray for you and the whole family." Lola's mom suggested to Grandpa.

"I don't think we need to ask him to come; it's not necessary." He said almost immediately. "You can just call him on phone on that day to pray."

"Grandpa, it's not right to call him on that day and ask him to pray for you. He should be properly informed." Lola said. "He's our pastor."

"I agree with Lola and my sister." Lola's aunt added. "Your pastor should be properly informed and invited. If he's not available, he will delegate someone to represent him."

"Yes." Lola's mother spoke again. "Also, I think that the Head of the Senior Adults' group in church should be made aware—"

Grandpa raised a hand to stop her. "No!"

"But you and mom are members of the group—"

"Yes, but I don't want us to invite people. You know my reason." Grandpa said firmly.

"Yes, I do, but we're talking about doing what is right here."

Grandpa eventually agreed, and Lola's mother was asked to inform the pastor and the Head of the Senior Adults' group.

Lola wondered what gift to give her grandfather. She was of the opinion that he had enough clothes; he even had clothes he was yet to wear as he didn't go out much, and she decided to discuss with her mother later, to know her opinion.

Shortly after they finished eating, Lola's aunt got up to leave, and the family saw her off.

When Lola was returning inside the house, she checked the time on her phone which she held in her hand- it was two-fifteen. She would need to start preparing for her outing.

In her room, she changed into her white bathrobe, took her towel, and went to the bathroom for a quick shower. Back in her room, she wore a long pink jacket and white camisole on jeans trousers which she had laid out on her bed. Her accessories were pink, and carrying her black handbag, she left the room.

"Are you going out?" Grandma asked. The woman was six years younger than her husband and had a small stature.

"Yes, Grandma."

"Okay, God bless you."

"Amen."

"Enjoy yourself." Her mother told her.

"I will. Thanks, Mom."

Outside, Lola entered her car, left for Lekan's house, and got there on time. She phoned Lekan to let her know that she had arrived, and Lekan went outside to meet her.

Lola looked at the younger lady as she approached her car. Lekan who was slim and slightly light skinned, wore a beautiful multicolored Ankara outfit that had short sleeves.

Lekan settled inside the car, and thanked Lola for coming to pick her up.

"You look good." She told Lola.

"Thanks. You look great too." Lola responded as she pulled back on the road.

"Thanks."

They located Dayo's house easily, and as Lola parked in front of the two-story building, she glanced at the clock on the dashboard, the time was four-ten. Lekan called Mercy on phone to let her know they had arrived, after which they got down from the car. Lola locked up the car, looked at the front flat on the first floor which Mercy had said was Dayo's, and saw some children playing at its balcony.

They entered the compound, walked up the stairs to the first floor, and found Mercy at the door to welcome them. She wore a pink knee-length gown. They greeted and followed her inside the apartment. Some people were there and just as Lola was wondering who was Dayo, a man came to meet them.

He and Lekan greeted familiarly.

"This is Dayo." Mercy introduced him to Lola, and they greeted.

With a broad smile, he appreciated them for coming, led them to two available seats, and they sat down, with Lekan on Lola's left side. Lola said hello to the lady on her right.

She glanced around and guessed that the place was a two-bedroom flat. She saw an elderly couple and guessed they must be Dayo's parents. Dayo's father was almost as tall as Dayo and had similar look, with some graying.

There were about twenty two people in the large living room. She looked at them and noticed a lady whom she guessed would be a teenager. Some of the men also looked young.

Shortly after, a man stood and called for everyone's attention. He announced that they were there to celebrate God's goodness and mercy: God kept them all, brought them into the New Year, and provided Dayo with the accommodation.

He asked a lady to lead them in praise and worship to God, and the lady asked everyone to stand. She led them in a series of songs for about ten minutes, after which another man prayed.

As everyone sat down, the man who gave the welcome address remained standing. He asked that they introduce themselves, and he got the ball rolling by telling them his name and profession.

Smiling, he said, "My name is Joshua. I am married, and that's my wife," he pointed at a lady, "What else?... I am a carpenter."

Some people laughed and a lady said, "A carpenter with a difference! CEO!"

As people introduced themselves, they mentioned their profession.

When it was Lekan's turn, she simply said, "My name is Lekan, and I'm Mercy's friend.

Lola followed suit. "I'm Lola, Mercy's cousin."

After the introduction, a lady was asked to bless the food. She did, and everyone said *Amen*.

People began to go to the kitchen to get their food which they brought into the living room to eat.

When the elderly couple and a younger couple got up to leave, Mercy and Dayo saw them off and returned inside.

"Let's go and get something to eat." Lekan told Lola.

"I'm not really hungry. You can go ahead." Lola said.

Lekan got up and went to the kitchen. When she returned to her seat beside Lola, Lola looked at her tray and saw what looked like peppersoup in one of the two bowls on it, and a can of juice.

"Is that peppersoup?" She asked.

"Yes. Mercy made it." Lekan said.

"Hmm, smells great. I'll have a little later."

The man who had the seat beside Lekan also returned and as he sat down, she saw Lekan's spoon drop to the floor. The man apologized, put his tray on his chair and returned to the kitchen to get another spoon which he gave to Lekan.

Mercy came to them and told Lekan that she'd like to see her when she finished eating.

Lekan said okay, Mercy left, and Lekan began to chat with the man beside her.

What am I doing here, Lord? Lola asked God under her breath as she glanced around. *This seems to be a waste of time.*

CHAPTER 3

The weather was warm that Wednesday afternoon. Two of John's cousins visited, and when the whole family was eating lunch, John was tempted to break his fast as he was hungry. However, he encouraged himself to hold on by reminding himself of the four things he was trusting God for in the year. He decided that he would eat at Dayo's get-together, to break his fast.

When the cousins eventually left, he went to his room to dress up, and returned to the living room.

"Your car or mine?" He asked Matthew and pointed at the key rack on a side of the living room wall.

"Mine, because I'll be going out after dropping you off." Matthew answered.

"Will Matthew come back to pick you up?" His father wanted to know.

"No, there's no need. I'm sure I'll get someone to give me a ride back." John answered.

He said goodbye to his parents and walked toward the front door.

Matthew also said goodbye, took his car keys, and followed John out of the house. There was no traffic and they soon got to Dayo's house.

John thanked his brother for the ride, used his left hand to open the door, and alighted from the car.

At the door of Dayo's apartment, he turned the doorknob, and when the door opened, he entered.

Dayo saw him immediately, smiled, and said something to the lady beside him, but when he noticed the bandage on John's arm, his facial expression changed as he exclaimed, "Wha-t?!"

He stood immediately and came to John. Four of the men in the room who knew John also came over to greet him. They all wanted to know what happened to his arm and he told them how he fell yesterday morning. They wished him speedy recovery and returned to their seats.

Mercy went to Dayo, and he introduced her to John.

****

Lola saw a man whose right hand was bandaged enter the room and saw Dayo and some men go to him. The tall man with low haircut, was dark skinned. When the men moved away, Mercy went to Dayo, and going by what Lola was seeing, she could tell that Dayo was introducing Mercy to the man.

Lola looked away from them, turned to Lekan, and said, "I think I'll just get something to eat."

"Okay."

Lola left for the kitchen.

****

John found a seat beside Wole, who was his friend. Wole's fiancé was beside him. John greeted them, sat down, and glanced at the faces of the people around. Only four of the ladies were unknown to him, and he wondered who among them was Mercy's friend.

He looked at his wristwatch—the time was now five-forty five—fifteen minutes to six when he would like to break his fast. He decided to ask about food now, to know what was available, and by the time he would get the food, it would be six—the time for him to eat.

He turned to Wole and said, "I'm hungry. Where's the food?"

"It's in the kitchen. Will you need help?"

John shook his head. "No, no. I'll be fine."

He stood and made his way to the kitchen.

A lady was there, standing by a counter, with a bowl in her hand. She glanced over her shoulder and when she saw him, she said, "Hi."

He looked at her and responded with his own *Hi*.

As she served peppersoup in a bowl for herself, John drew close to the counter. When she finished, she put the bowl on a tray, got a can of juice, spoon, and paper towel, and put them beside the bowl.

She turned to leave and then stopped. Looking at him, she asked, "Would you need help?"

"Er- I don't think so. I should be able to manage." He said and smiled a little. Knowing it was because of his bandaged arm, he added, "I had an accident yesterday."

"I'm sorry about that." She lowered the tray in her hand and took a plate.

Opening the trays, she asked John what he'd like to eat, and he told her.

"Thank you." He said, gratefully. "By the way, I'm John."

"I'm Lola." She said with a smile.

He thought that the smile made her look more beautiful. *Wait! Could she be the person that Dayo talked about*?

"Are you er … Mercy's friend?"

"Er … yes, she's my cousin."

Wow! This is the lady Dayo talked about, and I met her in the kitchen. What a coincidence, he thought. He took a closer look at her. She was tall, almost as tall as him and beautiful.

"I'm Dayo's friend. It's nice meeting you." He told her, smiling as his eyes took in her dressing.

"Nice meeting you too."

As she served his food, he observed her and told himself that not only was she beautiful, she was also nice.

She put the plate of food on a tray. John took a can of juice, put it on the tray and made to carry the tray.

"I can help you." She told him.

Wow, she really is a nice person! He smiled broadly and shook his head. "No, I can carry it. Thanks a lot."

She must be a Christian, for Dayo to want to introduce her to him. Well, he would like to get to know her better, he thought as he carried the tray with his left hand and followed her out of the kitchen.

They returned to the living room and went to their seats.

****

Lola sat down, and Lekan who had finished eating by then, took her tray to the kitchen, and returned to her seat.

****

John went straight to Dayo where he stood, and smiling broadly, he told Dayo, "I've met Mercy's friend."

"Where?"

"In the kitchen. She served me food. I like her, she's nice." He looked in the direction of Lola and added, "And I like the fact that she's slim and tall."

"Slim and tall?" Dayo asked with a frown. "Who are you talking about?"

"Mercy's friend. She said her name is Lola."

Realization dawned on Dayo. "Oh, Lola is her cousin. Lekan is her friend that I talked to you about."

"Oh!"

They laughed.

"I need to put my tray down." John said and went to his seat.

Dayo followed him.

He put his plate down on his chair and asked Dayo, "Where's the Lekan?"

"That's her beside Lola."

John laughed again. "They are sitting together. Wow! This is funny. Well, what about Lola? Is she married or engaged?"

"No, she's not. As a matter of fact, she's also trusting God for a man to marry. Mercy invited her."

Trusting God for a man to marry, John noted.

They moved a little away from Wole.

"Is Lola a Christian?" John asked Dayo.

"Yes."

"In that case, I'd like to get to know her better and see what God will do."

Dayo laughed and said, "Well, I still have to introduce you to Lekan. That's what I promised Mercy… so come on."

John laughed.

Dayo summoned Mercy and told her, "Will you get Lekan, please?"

John was laughing.

****

Lola was still eating when she saw Mercy coming in their direction, smiling a little.

Again, Mercy went to Lekan, and Lola heard her ask Lekan to come.

"Oh, I'm sorry. I forgot that you said you'd like to see me." Lekan responded.

"This is about something else." Mercy told Lekan.

Lekan stood and as she followed Mercy, Lola's eyes followed them.

****

As Lekan and Mercy walked toward John and Dayo, John was looking at Lekan. She was also beautiful. *Hmm.*

Dayo made the introductions. "Er, Lekan, meet John. He's one of my very good friends. John, this is Lekan, Mercy's friend."

As John shook hands with Lekan, he looked in the direction of Lola and saw her watching them.

He exchanged pleasantries with Lekan briefly, and then Lekan returned to her seat beside Lola.

****

Lola saw Mercy and Lekan go to Dayo who was standing with John. She saw them talking, and soon, Lekan returned to her seat. She didn't say anything to Lola, and Lola did not ask any question.

Whatever they had to do was none of her business, Lola reasoned.

****

John carried his tray and sat down, full of thoughts. Should he try to chat with Lekan, to please Dayo and Mercy, or try to get to know Lola better? *Hmm- what should I do, Lord*?

Well, he didn't think that Mercy and Dayo would greatly mind if he talked with Lola, after all, she was invited by Mercy. She was also Mercy's cousin, and single.

As he ate, he looked around and found that his gaze kept returning to Lola. He saw Lekan chatting with the man beside her, while Lola glanced around as she drank her peppersoup and juice.

After some minutes, he saw Lola getting up with her tray in her hand. *Is she going to the kitchen*?

When he saw her turn toward the kitchen, he stood with his tray in his hand and followed her.

CHAPTER 4

Lola entered the kitchen, took the empty can of juice, disposable bowl and spoon, and threw them in the trash bin. She was about to put the tray on the counter when someone entered the room, and she looked back.

When she saw John, she asked, "You need something?"

"Not really. Er- may I have your phone number?" He said, looking her straight in the eye. "I'd like to be able to call you to say hello."

He smiled and waited for her answer.

Surprised, she thought about the request for a few seconds. He sounded as though he meant it, and she considered him—he looked responsible, and mature, older than Dayo by her guess. He should be about her age.

She returned his smile and said, "Sure."

They exchanged phone numbers.

"Are you on Facebook?" He wanted to know.

"Yes."

"What's your name on Facebook?"

"Lola Thomas."

He typed on his phone.

"What's yours?"

"John thebeloved, two words."

"Okay." She did not think that she needed to write it down, she should be able to remember it. And she would definitely look him up to know more about him.

She decided to ask, "Are you a Christian?"

"Sure. Dayo and I attend the same church—*Great Grace Chapel.*"

"Oh, GGC. I know the church."

"Yes."

****

"What about you? Are you a Christian?" John asked to confirm what Dayo had told him.

Lola nodded as she washed her hands.

"Where do you worship?" He went on to ask.

"*Word of God Church,*" she said. Taking a paper towel, she wiped her hand, and threw the used paper towel in the waste bin.

"Good. Well, I'll keep in touch with you." He promised.

"Alright."

She walked toward the door, and he followed her out.

John returned to his seat to finish his food. He looked at Lekan and saw that she was still talking with the man beside her.

****

Just then, Dayo's friend, Jim, stood in the center of the room, called for everyone's attention, and asked the people who were standing to sit.

He said that aside being there to celebrate the goodness of God, they were also there for fellowship and that fellowship was an important part of the true believers' walk with God as it had several benefits.

"In fellowship, we show one another how to live for God, someone learns something positive while everyone gains encouragement and strength, and God is glorified."

He read Hebrews chapter ten, verses twenty four and twenty five.

Let us think of ways to motivate one another toward acts of love and good works. And let us not neglect our meeting together, as some people do, but encourage one another, especially now that the day of his return is drawing near.

Jim went on. "As we are here, Jesus is here because His word says that where two or three gather in His name, He will be with them. Christian fellowship also helps us to build lasting relationships. For example, I met Dayo at a fellowship some years back. We became friends and I treasure our friendship."

One of the men went to him, whispered in his ear, and returned to his seat.

Jim continued. "And so, this is a Christian gathering, and before you leave this place, try to get to know at least a person better. But now, it is time to encourage one another according to First Corinthians chapter fourteen, verse twenty six. I'll read the NLT and it says, '*Well, my brothers and sisters, let's summarize. When you meet together, one will sing, another will teach, another will tell some special revelation God has given, one will speak in tongues, and another will interpret what is said. But everything that is done must strengthen all of you.*' And so, if the Holy Spirit drops something in your heart, let's hear it."

When Dayo indicated that he'd like to talk, Jim called him. Dayo stood to talk while Jim went to his seat.

Dayo said that a Scripture had been coming to his mind since morning, and as he talked about it to encourage everyone, Lola felt that she should also talk, more so as she was a pastor. Encouraging people to get closer to God was her calling.

Taking her phone, she opened her notes to check some of her prepared sermons, to see the one she could use to encourage the gathering for about five minutes. She decided on one, and as she thought about it, she changed her mind. She did not have to talk. She would just listen to what others had to say and be blessed.

With that decided, she put her phone away, and listened.

****

After Dayo, two people shared the scriptures in their hearts, and then Lekan stood to talk. She began by saying that divine purposes would be different just as people were different.

As she talked, John looked at her. *Should I try to chat with her after this session and get her phone number?* He considered the idea but decided against it. He did not think that he should, not after exchanging phone numbers with Lola. That wouldn't speak well of him, he thought. It would make him seem like a lousy person.

Lekan was still speaking. "Some are called to be pastors, some are evangelists, some will be singers, encouragers, and so on. As the last speaker said, everyone should discover his or her calling, accept it, and be faithful in it."

John nodded in agreement. He could play keyboard and sing very well, but his ministry was to reach out to teenagers.

****

When Lekan finished and sat down, another person stood to talk.

Lola checked the time on her phone, turned to Lekan, and asked, “Can we leave when this person is through?”

Lekan shrugged. “It’s okay.”

As soon as the person finished, Mercy raised her hand, and she was called.

Lola didn’t think that they could leave now, and she tapped Lekan to get her attention.

“Yes?”

“Let's leave after Mercy's talk.”

“Alright.”

The moment Mercy stopped, Lola carried her handbag.

Lekan did the same, said goodnight to the man beside her, and they stood.

****

When Lola and Lekan carried their handbags and stood, John looked at them, with the hope that Lola would look in his direction so he could wave at her, but she did not. Lekan did however, but before he could raise his left hand to wave at her, she had looked away. Mercy got up to see them off.

John turned to Wole, “Did you come in your car? I’ll need a ride, please. I didn’t come in my car because of my arm.”

“Yes, sure. No problem.”

“Thank you.”

****

As the three ladies descended the stairs, Lola and Lekan teased Mercy about Dayo, and laughed. Outside the gate, Lola unlocked her car with the remote and she and Lekan got inside.

When Lola started the car, Mercy waved and told them, “I'll talk to both of you later.”

As soon as Lola pulled away, Lekan asked her, “So, what do you think about the whole thing?”

Lola chuckled. “I don't know what to say. Maybe I shouldn't have gone. Some of them looked young!”

Lekan responded with a smile, “I feel the same way. I don’t think anything was achieved.”

“Well, we had fellowship.”

“And we ate, so it wasn’t a complete waste of time.” Lekan added.

They laughed.

“A guy named John asked for my name and phone number though, but that was all.” Lola said.

Lekan gave Lola a sharp look and asked, “Did you say John?!”

“Yes, the guy with the bandage on his arm.”

“Oh wow!” Lekan exclaimed under her breath and returned her gaze to her front.

“I saw you talking with that guy beside you.” Lola said and chuckled, not realizing the impact that what she had said was having on Lekan.

“We were just making small talks. He collected my phone number too.” Lekan revealed dully. “He’s a Youth Corper.” That was what NYSC members were called.

“A Youth Corper,” Lola repeated and laughed. “He might not be older than twenty three years.”

"Probably." Lekan said and shrugged without interest.

"It is well." Lola added.

Lola continued talking, but when she realized that Lekan was not responding much, she glanced sideways at her and noticed a slight frown on her face.

"Is everything okay?"

"Yes." Lekan answered and smiled a little.

Lola returned her gaze to the road.

There was silence for some seconds then Lekan asked her, "When did you talk with John? I didn't see you together."

"In the kitchen." Lola answered.

Lekan's eyebrows shot up. "In the kitchen?!"

"Yes." Lola said and smiled. "I met him in the kitchen when I went to get something to eat, and when I returned my tray to the kitchen, he came there to ask for my name and number."

"Hmm, interesting."

"It is, can you imagine?" Lola laughed and continued making small talks.

When they reached Lekan's house, Lekan thanked Lola, alighted from the car, and went inside the house.

Lola did not move immediately. Feeling like listening to some good music on her way home, she took her phone, and went on YouTube. She searched for Rev. Oyenike Areogun's songs, tapped on the one at the top, and put the phone down on the passenger seat as it began to play. She engaged the gear and as she pulled away, music filled the inside of the car. She joined the woman of God to sing to worship God.

Final Authority, Supreme Authority, Highest Authority,
I bow before You, Lord...
Higher than the highest, Greater than the greatest,
Bigger than the biggest, Mightier than the mightiest...
Nothing is beyond my Father,
No one is above my God,
Nothing can be above You, Lord,
I bow before You, Lord...

At home, Lola's grandparents were in the living room with Seun Alabi and her visitors. Lola greeted them and went to her room. After changing her clothes, she went to the kitchen to get food which she brought to her room to eat.

Sitting on her bed with the tray of food beside her, she took her phone.

What did John say his name on Facebook was? *John thebeloved*? She typed the name on Facebook, and three accounts came up. The profile picture on the first account was that of a couple and two children. Could this be his account? Was he married? She clicked on the name to see if it was John's account, and found that it wasn't.

A man was in the profile picture of the second account, and she thought that he was the one in the picture. She opened the account to confirm—yes, it was the face she saw at the event quite alright.

Going through his posts, she thought that he was a committed Christian. She saw some of his pictures and smiled. *Not bad.*

Well, let's see if he gets in touch. If he did, she would ask him questions so that she would know his stand with God.

A woman introduced a man to her last year. The woman had assured her that the man was a Christian but when the man phoned her and she began to ask him questions, he confessed that he was not a committed Christian and did not go to church regularly. When she told the woman about the man's confession, the woman said she should not let that discourage her as the man would not stop her from going to church if she married him.

No way! Lola had thought. She would not fall into that trap, it would be wrong to marry such a man.

"Thank you, Ma, but no. I don't want a husband who will not stop me from going to church, I want a husband who has a relationship with God and will serve God together with me." Lola had responded nicely, but firmly.

Before Lola ended her call to the woman that day, she thanked the woman again because she knew that the woman meant well and was only trying to help her.

Lola tapped on WhatsApp App to see if John's phone number would come up, but just then, her door swung open and her mother stood there.

"How did the event go?" She asked Lola.

"It went well, thank you." Lola said without elaborating further. "Have your visitors gone?"

"Yes. Did anything of interest happen?"

"Not really. A man exchanged phone numbers with me, but that was all." Lola answered.

"It is well."

Lola changed the line of discussion and asked, "What do you plan to give Grandpa for his birthday?"

"Thanks for reminding me, I was going to discuss it with you." Seun Alabi sat beside her daughter on the bed. "I know someone who can do a portrait painting of him. What do you think?"

"That's good, but that usually takes time to do."

"I asked the person and he said it can be ready if he starts on it tomorrow."

"If it can be ready then I think it's okay."

"I'm thinking of a full-length portrait painting, from both of us."

"How much will it cost?" Lola asked.

Her mother told her the amount.

"Okay. You can give him advance payment so he can start. I'll transfer the money to you tomorrow."

Her mother thanked her.

When her mother left, Lola looked John up on WhatsApp and found him.

Few minutes after ten, she received Mercy's call.

"Are you back at home?" Mercy wanted to know.

"Yes, and thanks for inviting me." She said politely. "What about you?"

"Yes, I'm back at home, and I should thank you for coming. So, what do you think? Did you enjoy yourself?" Mercy asked Lola meaningfully.

Lola laughed a little and said, "Yes, I did enjoy myself, but… I don't know what to say. Maybe I shouldn't have attended."

What?! "Why?" Mercy asked.

"Some of the people looked young! I'm sure that one of the girls is even a teenager."

"Not all of them are young." Mercy countered. "One of Dayo's friends, Joshua, is married, and he was there with his wife. Jim and Wole were there with their fiancé."

"Well, a guy named John took my phone number." Lola said, chuckled, and added, "I enjoyed the fellowship and peppersoup though."

"Well, I prayed for you and Lekan." Mercy told her.

"Thank you."

"Anyway, one must keep on trying, you know. You need to keep going out and meeting people. God will eventually lead you to your own man."

Does she think that I don't go out or don't know what to do? Lola thought. "Thanks, dear cousin." She said simply.

Few minutes after, she received a chat from her friend, Sarah.

We will be back on Sunday evening. I'll pop in at your office on Monday afternoon, and then you can tell me all about the get-together.

Ok, great! Will expect you.

****

The get-together ended at eight that evening with closing prayer. When the others began to clean up Dayo's place, John joined them, using his left hand to do what he could. It did not take long, and by eight-forty five, they had finished and were out of the house. He joined Wole and his fiancé in Wole's car, and they left.

At home, his parents had visitors. He greeted them and went to his room. Some minutes after, Matthew phoned him. He wanted to know if John was still at Dayo's house so he could pick him up, and John said he was back at home.

When the visitors left, he left his room to join his parents in the living room, and shortly after, Matthew arrived. At about ten, their parents retired to their room.

"So, how was the event?" Matthew asked.

John chuckled. "It was okay, it went well."

"Did Dayo introduce the lady to you?"

"Yes, he did, but something funny happened." John laughed, and as he told Matthew about Lola, he could still see her smiling face in his mind. He liked her smile, especially when it was directed at him.

"Somehow, I like her." He added.

"Is she a Christian?" Matthew asked.

"Yes. She said so, and Dayo confirmed it."

"Well, try to know more about her."

"Yes, I intend to do that. I will ask Dayo about her." John said.

But almost immediately, he wondered – *why should I do that? What's special about Lola*? The churches he attended in Lagos and Akure were filled with single Christian women who were both beautiful and wonderful. He was not in love with any of them, but should he consider one of them? *Hmm.*

He decided to forget about Lola; he would not ask Dayo about her. But what about his promise to her to keep in touch? He must fulfill his promise being a Christian, he reasoned. *Okay, I'll contact her to say hello, but won't try to pursue her*, he resolved.

However, by the time he entered his room, he had forgotten all about his resolve, and taking his phone, he looked Lola up on Facebook. Her last post was about Kathryn Kuhlman, and it showed that the post was the nineteenth one on the woman. He knew the woman's story and he began to read the post.

When he was through, he began to scroll down Lola's page, searching for her first post about Kathryn Kuhlman. He found it and began to read.

Excerpts from the book—Kathryn Johanna Kuhlman, Daughter of Destiny.

It has been estimated that during her 50 years of ministry, Kathryn Johanna Kuhlman witnessed to over 100 million people and wherever she went, astounding miracles followed her!! Hers is a story of love, bitter heartache, rejection, and finally... triumph!!!

He scrolled up and read Day two and Day three which were about Kathryn Kuhlman's birth, name, and family.

He went up to Day four, and began to read:

Kathryn had just turned 14 years when the Rev. Hummel, a Baptist evangelist came to Concordia to hold a 2-week revival service at the tiny Methodist Chapel.

While the Evangelist was giving out an invitation for the people to give their hearts to Jesus, Kathryn began to weep. At the time, she didn't realize that it was God's Holy Spirit dealing with her heart. The weeping became intense, so intense that she began to shake. Kathryn dropped her hymnbook into the rack at the back of the chair in front of her and staggered down to the front of the little wooden chapel, collapsing into the front pew, with her head in her hands weeping uncontrollably. Her loud sobbing could be heard all over the chapel. The good people of Concordia who were there that morning were amazed to see that sight as they were not used to seeing such emotionalism in their chapel meetings and could not understand what had got hold of 'nice' Kathryn Kuhlman. But like many others, Kathryn had come under the convicting power of the Holy Spirit, had seen her own unworthiness in the light of the 'Worthy One', Jesus, and, like many before her, had come to the foot of the old rugged cross in true, heartfelt repentance of sin, and become washed in the blood of the Lamb. And, like the many who had trod the same paths before her, Kathryn Johanna Kuhlman would never be the same again.

He continued reading until he got to the last post which was today.

Captivated all over again by how greatly God used the woman, he went online to read more about her. He found several articles about her, and about some other men and women of God. Changing his mind, he decided to read about Kenneth E. Hagin, and Oral Roberts, American preachers, and didn't sleep until around one in the morning.

On Thursday morning, he told his mother that he would like to buy some things to take to Akure, and when his brother was ready to drive him to the clinic for treatment, their mother went with them so she could assist John to get the things he wanted.

CHAPTER 5

On Friday, Dayo called John to say that he would visit him later in the day. Guessing that Dayo might want to discuss Lola with him, he began to lecture his heart to do the right thing and dismiss Lola. He would try not to discuss her with Dayo.

When Dayo came, he asked John about his accident again, and John explained in detail.

"I was surprised when I didn't see you in church for Cross-over Service." Dayo said. "I didn't know that you had an accident."

"It was not because of the accident; I went with my family to their church."

"Oh, I see." Dayo said, and then asked about Lola. "It seems you like her,"

John laughed.

Dayo smiled. "Why didn't you try to talk with Lekan?"

"I wasn't certain about doing that, and when I'm not sure about something, I'm careful."

Dayo nodded in understanding.

"Also, I didn't want to talk to her after asking Lola for her name and phone number. They sat together; they might discuss and if they found out that I got the phone numbers of both of them, that could make me look irresponsible and bad." He explained.

"That's true." Dayo agreed.

"It seems they are friends, they left together that day."

"I don't know if they are close, but Mercy invited both of them, and they came together."

"It's a good thing that I didn't make a move concerning Lekan."

"You're right. So, have you contacted Lola?"

"No, no." John said and laughed.

He hadn't forgotten his resolve and the lecture he gave his heart earlier in the day but now, his heart seemed to have a mind of its own and refused to obey him and he found himself saying, "I'd like to ask you about her."

"What do you wish to know?"

John smiled. "Just tell me what you know about her."

"To be honest, I don't know much." Dayo confessed. "It's Lekan that I know a little about."

Dayo went on to tell him how the two ladies came to be at the event.

"I see."

"I can ask Mercy about Lola though." Dayo suggested.

"Okay."

"When are you going back to Akure?" Dayo asked.

"Tomorrow."

"How time flies! Your two-week Christmas break is over." Dayo commented. "How will you go back to Akure? What about your car?"

"My brother will drive me down in my car and board a bus back to Lagos."

"Why don't you call your office, tell them about the accident, and ask for a few days more to get back in shape?"

John shook his head. "No, I have things to do there. I'll be fine, I'll manage."

When John was seeing Dayo off, he asked, "When are you likely to ask Mercy about Lola?"

"I'll ask her today and call you to let you know whatever she says." Dayo promised.

In the evening, Dayo phoned him. "I've talked with Mercy, and she said that Lola is twenty nine years old, works in a bank, and is a pastor in her church."

"A pastor? Wow!"

They laughed.

"So, she's unattached?"

"Yes. Mercy said that she was engaged to be married sometime ago, but the man died."

John exclaimed, surprised. "Died?!"

"Yes."

John exclaimed again. "That's a big one!"

"It is."

"How long ago was that?"

"Mercy didn't tell me." Dayo answered.

"Okay, thanks."

"So, are you going to call Lola?"

"I will definitely contact her to say hello." John answered, paused, and then added, "Well, we'll see how it goes."

He considered contacting Lola that evening but counseled himself to wait. He had a lot to do, and a lot was on his mind now as he would be traveling tomorrow. He would wait until he was back in Akure and could think clearly to know what exactly to do.

Early on Saturday morning, John's stuff was put in his official car, and by eight-thirty, he was heading back to Akure with Matthew behind the wheel. They stopped on the way to buy roasted corn to eat, and by one in the afternoon, they reached their destination in Akure.

There were two identical bungalows in the large compound, owned by two brothers who were identical twins, and each bungalow had two apartments with two bedrooms, that were rented out.

John got down and opened the gate so that Matthew could bring the car inside the compound. He asked Matthew to park in front of the bungalow on the right, Matthew did so, and John closed the black painted gate.

Matthew got down, carried some items, and followed John to the apartment at the back of the bungalow which John shared with his colleague.

John unlocked the door of the two-bedroom apartment, and when they entered, Matthew glanced around. The living room had a chocolate sofa and loveseat set, a center table, and three wall décors.

John looked around too—the living room looked exactly as he had left it; a small Bible was on the center table, and three books and a bookstore receipt were on the sofa. His colleague, Adams, left before him for the Christmas holiday, and there was no sign that he had returned from Ibadan in Oyo state, where his family lived.

"Where do you want me to put these?" Matthew asked him.

"Put them down by that door, please." John pointed at his bedroom door.

Matthew did so, and they went outside to get the remaining items in the car. Back in the house, the items were put by John's door and while Matthew ate a little from the food that John brought from home and drank chilled Coca Cola which he got from the refrigerator, John moved around. He opened the living room windows wide, turned on the TV and two ceiling fans in the large room, before unlocking his bedroom door.

The neat room had a queen size bed which was at the center of the longest wall in the room, a freestanding mirror, a closet, a white ceiling fan, a black steel folding chair, and a black table, among other things.

He opened the room's windows, turned on the ceiling fan, and then returned to the living room. Taking his phone, he called his parents to make them know that he and Matthew reached Akure safely, and that Matthew would leave soon.

When Matthew finished eating, he wanted to take the used items to the kitchen, but John told him not to bother.

"You need to leave now so you can reach Lagos on time." John said.

He told Matthew how to get to the bus station, and Matthew left.

John locked the front door, put away the things he brought from Lagos, cleaned his room, and then sat down in the living room to eat. Afterward, he turned the TV off, showered, and went to his room to sleep.

A loud sound suddenly woke him up. Wondering what it was, he listened and when he heard voices and movement coming from the living room, he knew that his colleague, Adams, must have returned. He glanced at the wall clock; the time was six-forty six in the evening.

Taking his phone, he called Matthew to know where he was, and Matthew said that he was still on the way. He asked Matthew to let him know when he got home.

Getting up from bed, he laced his fingers together, raised his hands over his head, and stretched. He wore a shirt on his pair of trousers, took his phone, and left his room.

Adams was in the living room with one of their neighbors, and when they saw his arm, they were surprised. They exchanged greetings and then John sat down to chat with them.

He was still in the living room an hour and a half after when Matthew called to inform him that he had gotten home.

In the morning of the next day, as John got ready to go to church, Lola was not far from his mind, and he decided to call her in the afternoon. He had promised to call her, and he would, but was God involved? Should he consider one of the ladies in his church? He asked God to take control and make him know in which direction he should go.

His colleague dropped him off in church before going to his own church. When the service ended, John trekked to a nearby restaurant where he bought food, and then he called a cab that brought him back home.

After lunch in his room, he looked at the time, it was two-fifty five. Lola might still be in church. He would call her at four or forty-thirty, she should be at home by then.

At about four-twenty, he phoned Lola, but it was not answered, and he sent a message to her on WhatsApp.

This is John, we met on Wednesday.

Putting the phone down, he dismissed Lola from his mind, and left the room to get water to drink. Within minutes, he was back in his room with a small bottle of water in his hand. He opened it, drank a little, and as he put the bottle down on his table, his eyes went to his list of prayer requests, the four things he would like to achieve in the year.

He took the paper and laying on his back in bed, he considered the list.

Number one, *a better job*. He was already taking steps concerning this.

Two, *to establish an additional stream of income*. He had been thinking about this, but he was not yet sure of what exactly to do.

His mind went to the pastor's sermon in church today. The pastor had talked about the fact that God would use a person's skill or the gift in a person to raise the person.

John could write poems and had written some in High School and University. What about writing some and turning them into a book, or sell them to magazines or individuals who might be interested in them?

He also played keyboard very well and played it in the church in Akure. He was the only instrumentalist in the Akure church that was not on the church's payroll. Should he approach the pastor and ask to be paid salary?

He thought about it briefly and shook his head. Asking the church where he worshipped to pay him salary for playing keyboard during service did not sound right. If he would not ask to be paid for teaching the teenagers in the church, then he should not ask to be paid for playing keyboard. He would not condemn the other instrumentalists who were being paid however, some of them might depend on the salary.

He would have to look for other ways to make money.

What about teaching people how to play keyboard? Hmm. Putting the paper in his hand down, he considered the idea. This was something that he could easily do on the side after work, or at weekends on days that there would be no service in the church. This could work and he could start making money right away but how should he go about it? How would he get students? He would also need access to a keyboard as he did not own one.

The more he thought about this, the more it appealed to him. Another thing occurred to him, he could have private students, teach in a school, or an academy, but how much would he charge? *Holy Spirit, lead me in Jesus' name.*

Taking his phone, he went online and began to search for more information about this business idea. He would also like to know how much others in the business charged in this town.

"John?" Adams called him.

"Yes?"

He got up, took the bottle of water and his phone, and went to the living room. Adams wanted to discuss a client's matter with him, and he sat down.

He was still in the living room talking with Adams around seven in the evening when Lola's call came in.

"Hello," he said as he got up to go to his room, with the phone held to his ear.

"Hello, John. I'm sorry I missed your call; I was in church then." Lola said.

He wanted to say… *Dayo told me that you're a pastor*, but he thought it unnecessary, and he bit it back. Besides, she might not be pleased to know that Dayo told him some things about her.

He said instead, "I guessed as much. I just wanted to say hello."

"Thank you."

He entered his bedroom, closed the door, and sat on the chair. "What time does Sunday service end in your church?"

"It usually ends around one in the afternoon, but we had a guest minister today who took some time. And afterward, I had to meet with some people." She explained.

"Oh, okay."

"Did you go to church today?" She asked, to know if he was a committed Christian.

"Yes, I did." He answered.

"So, how was church?" She pressed on.

"It was great."

She remembered that he said he worshipped at *Great Grace Chapel,* and said, "I sometimes watch Pastor Dave on TV. He's a man of God."

"He is, definitely." He confirmed. "I joined the church about eleven years ago, but I worship at *Peace Chapel* when I'm in Akure."

"Akure in Ondo state?!"

"Yes, that's where I work."

"Oh, I see. So, when are you going back to Akure?"

"I'm there now, I returned yesterday." He said.

"Where do you work?" She wanted to know.

"I work at the regional office of *Intent Home.* We sell home and wall décor."

Intent Home?! Is he even a University graduate? "Did you study Marketing or something related, in the University?" She asked, to hear what he would say.

"I studied Business Administration."

He's a University graduate, good. "Which University?"

He told her.

"Well, I guess that working in a regional office comes with some benefits, right?"

"Well, yes, but in this case, it's not really working for me, and I hope to leave soon." He revealed.

"Why is it not working for you?"

"Well, it's a one-man business, and some of the things I was promised when I joined the organization about six years ago are yet to be done. Er- and of course, the salary could be much better. I have an official car and accommodation which I share with my colleague, but that's about it."

"I see,"

He added with a chuckle, "And well, like my colleague says, another benefit is that we don't have a manager breathing down our neck, and we don't have to dress up as much as we'd be expected to, at the head office."

She smiled.

"But I need more."

"Yeah," she agreed.

"I need to move on, and I think that I'd like to return to Lagos."

"That's fine. Have you started making moves concerning another job?"

"Yes, I contacted some people when I was in Lagos." He answered.

"I pray everything turns out right for you, in Jesus' name."

"Amen."

She asked, "How's your arm? Hope it's healing well,"

"Yes, thank you. I'll be seeing my doctor here in Akure, tomorrow. The bandage should be removed soon, hopefully." He said. "So, what do you do? Where do you work?"

"I work at Dominion Bank."

Knowing that the bank had several branches in Lagos, he asked, "Which of the branches?"

She told him.

They talked for about fifteen minutes more, and he promised to call her again soon before saying goodnight.

He had enjoyed talking to her. His phone showed that he spent thirty eight minutes on the phone with her, which surprised him and made him smile. He had thought that the call would be brief. *Lead me, Lord.*

****

When the call ended, Lola phoned Mercy.

After exchanging greetings, she said, "John called me."

"John—Dayo's friend?"

"Yes." She laughed. "I missed his call in the afternoon and returned the call this evening."

"Wow! That's nice." Mercy said. "So, how did it go? What did he say?"

"Well, we were just making some small talks, trying to know each other better. He said he works in Akure."

"Yes, Dayo told me that he works in the regional office of a company." Mercy confirmed. "Dayo knows him very well."

Okay, good, Lola thought.

The call lasted about eight minutes.

At about two-thirty on Monday afternoon, Sarah came to the bank to see Lola.

"So, how was your honeymoon?"

Sarah laughed. "It was awesome! We had some amazing moments even though we did not leave the hotel."

"Wow!"

Sarah laughed again. "We snapped tons of pictures, watched some Christian movies, and reminisced about our wedding ceremonies- who came and what happened. A Pentecostal church held services in one of the halls in the hotel, so we joined them for some of the services, and we were blessed. That was just perfect for us—we were on our honeymoon, yet we attended church."

She brought out her phone and as she showed Lola some of the pictures, they had a good laugh.

They chatted for a few minutes about Sarah's wedding ceremony, and afterward, Sarah wanted to know about the get-together and Lola told her about John.

Opening WhatsApp on her phone, she tapped on John's profile picture, and gave her phone to Sarah. "That's him."

Sarah enlarged the picture.

"He called me yesterday." Lola added and told Sarah about their discussion.

As Sarah returned the phone, she said that if God was involved, they would soon know.

CHAPTER 6

That Monday, John resumed at work. It was a busy day, and he couldn't leave to go to the hospital until around six in the evening.

By Wednesday, he had decided to become a keyboard teacher and how much to charge monthly. He had also found and arranged with a man who had a piano and a keyboard in his studio. The next thing would be to let people know about it, so he could get students, and he decided to use word of mouth and social media.

At home in the evening, he started by telling his colleague and neighbors, asking them to please tell others that they knew someone who could teach them to play keyboard. He also announced it on his social media handles: Learn to play piano / keyboard.

While on Facebook, he sent a friend request to Lola. He went on WhatsApp, tapped on her name and saw that she was online. He returned to Facebook to send a message to a friend, and just then, he was notified by Facebook that Lola had accepted his friend request.

When he was through with Facebook, he called Lola and while they were talking, Lola heard her grandmother calling her.

"Hold on, my grandma is calling me," she told John and then muted the phone to answer her grandmother.

Within a minute, she unmuted the phone and said, "Hello,"

"Hello." John responded.

"Sorry, my grandma needed something." She explained to him.

"Are you through with her or would you need some minutes?"

"No, I'm through."

"Is she your paternal or maternal grandmother?"

"Maternal."

"Do you live together?"

"Yes, my grandfather is also here."

"How old are they?"

"Grandpa is turning eighty soon, and Grandma is seventy four." She revealed.

He told her that his paternal grandparents were late while his maternal grandparents lived in Delta.

"My mom is from Delta, but my dad is Yoruba." He revealed.

"Oh, I see."

He went on, "I have two brothers: one older, one younger. The older one lives in Germany with his family and my younger brother is a chartered accountant."

"A chartered accountant? That's good. Is he married?"

"No, not yet." He answered.

"Is he in Lagos?"

"Yes, he lives with my parents."

"You don't have a sister?" She asked.

"No. What about you?" He was curious about her too.

"I'm an only child." She said.

"Wow! I hear that such children get spoilt." He teased.

She laughed. "Not in my case. My grandmother made sure that I was not spoilt. She ensured that I did my share of chores. If I did not, she would pull and twist my ears, or use one of her stirring rods in the kitchen to beat me."

He laughed.

Soon, they were talking about church, and he said that he played keyboard in the Akure church.

She told him how she became a Christian, and that she was the evangelism leader of her campus fellowship, in her final year in university.

"When were you ordained a pastor?"

"Last year." She said.

She added that she held a monthly Saturday program to disciple some teenage girls in her neighborhood.

"Oh, that's great! I'm also involved with the teenagers in the church in Lagos and here in Akure." He said excitedly. "I'm one of the teachers, but it's more than that for me—it's a ministry."

They began to talk about their experiences, and he revealed that he became born again at the age of fourteen.

"I was also a teenager when I gave my life to Christ, I was seventeen." She told him.

"Teens ministry is absolutely essential." He said. "There's a great need for it. Some decisions that can affect life are made during the teenage years."

She agreed with him.

He shared with her some of the struggles and challenges he faced as a teenager, before and after he became a Christian, and how he overcame them.

"Does the fellowship hold in your house?" He asked.

"No. There's a nice small hall in the neighborhood which we use. The owner is my mom's friend, and she allows us to use it."

Has the Lord brought John into my life for a reason? She wondered as they talked.

They ended up talking for about fifty minutes, and he had enjoyed every minute of it!

Did I hear a bit of excitement in her voice, or is it my imagination? He wondered.

When he woke up in the morning of the next day, he checked his phone after prayers and found that some people had responded to his post about the keyboard lessons. They wanted more information, and he quickly responded before getting up to prepare for work.

He called Lola again on Saturday, and on Tuesday, she called him to know how he was doing. She said that she saw his post about teaching keyboard lessons, and he explained that he'd just decided to do it on the side.

"Have you started it?"

"No, but two people are showing interest already."

****

Lola was about to close at work on Friday evening when she received a text message from her mother to inform her that the portrait had been delivered and had been kept in Lola's room. In her room at home, Lola checked the portrait- it was good. Her mother had also put wrapping paper and sealing tape on her table.

Before she slept that night, she wrapped the portrait, and selected the clothes she would wear for her grandfather's birthday the next day.

On Saturday morning, she woke up early to clean her room, and afterward, went to the kitchen to prepare breakfast while the housekeeper cleaned the house.

After breakfast, Grandpa who wore a shirt on shorts, returned to the bedroom while Grandma remained in the living room. Lola loaded the refrigerator with bottles of water, juice, and soft drinks such as Coca Cola, and at about one in the afternoon, the food caterer employed by Seun Alabi delivered the food for the occasion.

Shortly after, the birthday cake was delivered by a man. The white-gold-black cake had a glittery gold topper that read *Happy 80th, Grandpa, Loved & Blessed.* Seun Alabi put the beautiful round cake on a table in a corner of the living room that had been decorated with a few gold and white balloons.

Seun Alabi's immediate younger sister and her family were the first to arrive at about two in the afternoon, and Grandma went inside the bedroom to inform Grandpa. Soon both of them emerged from the room. Grandpa had changed into a simple but nice *buba* and *sokoto* attire. The *buba* was a shirt with a loose-fitting neck that reached halfway down his thighs while the *sokoto* was the trousers. Grandma wore a gown that made her look dignified.

"*Happy birthday to you, happy birthday to you, happy birthday to you, Grandpa, happy birthday to you.*" The newcomers sang and began to hug Grandpa one by one.

Lola considered her grandfather as he greeted the family members and thought that he seemed a little frail. Her grandparents were definitely getting older, and she wondered how she would feel when they eventually passed on. She would miss them, and she prayed under her breath that they would live longer and see her get married and have children.

It was a wonderfully warm afternoon and by three-forty when the pastor of *Word of God Church* and his wife arrived, the living room was full and some of Lola's cousins sat on chairs at the balcony. Christian music was playing in the background while a hired female photographer took pictures of the celebrant and captured every activity and everyone present. At four, the pastor told Lola's mother that they would have to start, and she asked the people at the balcony to come inside.

Sarah and her husband arrived, and few minutes after, Mercy came in, carrying a gift bag. She greeted everyone, hugged her grandparents, and went to stand beside her cousins.

The pastor's wife got up to say the opening prayer, and everyone seated, stood up. Only Grandpa remained seated, with his walking stick beside him.

After the brief prayer, Lola led them to praise and worship God for some minutes, and then the pastor gave a brief exhortation which was followed by prayer for the celebrant and his family.

****

John called Lola around four-thirty that Saturday afternoon, but the call was not answered. He sent a message to her on WhatsApp.

I called. How are you?

He put his phone down and hoped she would call him back soon. She was probably in church.

He began to think about the busy life of a pastor. *Hmm. I like her, and I'd like to see where this friendship is heading, but is marriage to a pastor what I really want?* He had no problem getting married to a woman with a calling, after all, he was like a pastor to the teens in his church, but he would need to be sure of what he wanted because marriage was not a child's play.

****

When the pastor finished, the birthday song was sung for Grandpa, and then he cut the cake with his wife beside him.

The pastor gave Grandpa a gift and said that he and his wife would need to take their leave. Grandpa's family thanked the couple for coming and for the gift.

People began to go to Grandpa to take pictures with him and those who had gifts presented them to him.

Lola went to the kitchen, carried the food and drinks that her mother had packed for the pastor, and together with her mother, saw the couple off.

On her way back inside the house, she brought out her phone from the pocket of the floral dress with puff sleeves that she wore. It had been vibrating inside her pocket during the pastor's exhortation, but she had ignored it.

When she checked and saw John's missed call and message, she smiled and began to type.

Just seeing your message. I'm kind of busy now. I'll call you back later.

She sent it and he responded immediately.

Okay.

Back in the house, food and drinks were being served, and soon, everyone was eating, drinking, talking, and laughing. Some of the teenagers returned to the balcony.

"Let's quickly talk." Mercy told Lola.

They carried their plates of food and drinks and went into Lola's bedroom.

"I thought you'd come with your siblings and cousins," Lola told Mercy.

"I couldn't." Mercy responded. "Dayo moved into his apartment today, and I had to be there to assist him. Some of his friends were there too."

"Where's Stella? Will she come?"

"She will." Mercy answered. "She and her fiancé had to see some people today in preparation for their wedding."

"Oh, I see. The wedding is in April, right?"

"Yes, April 25. The invitation card should be out soon."

Lola smiled. "April 25- that's the day after my birthday."

"Yes, and that reminds me—you're turning thirty—what's your plan? How do you intend to celebrate it?"

Lola shrugged. "I haven't given it much thought yet, but it's not going to be anything elaborate- that's certain. I may just invite some close friends and family, that's all."

"Okay."

Lola added, "It falls on a Friday and Stella's wedding is on Saturday, so, if there's going to be a celebration, it will have to be on Sunday."

"Alright, let me know whatever you decide on time, so I can save the date."

"Okay."

"So, how are you and John? Are you still communicating?" Mercy asked.

Lola laughed. "Yes. He even called me this afternoon, although I couldn't answer it because that was when my pastor was preaching. I'll call him later."

They continued talking and then Lola asked, "When are you and Dayo likely to get married?"

"We're looking at October."

"This year?"

"Yes." Mercy said and laughed.

"Oh, wow! That's good."

"He has a job and his own apartment. I also have a job. We don't want an unnecessarily long courtship." Mercy explained.

"That's right."

Just then, Mercy's phone began to ring. She looked at it and said, "Stella,"

She picked the call, "Hello, Stella,"

Stella wanted to know if Mercy was still at Grandpa's place and Mercy said yes.

"I'm on my way."

"Okay, I'll be waiting for you." Mercy told Stella before they ended the call.

Lola and Mercy talked a little more and then returned to the living room to join the other cousins who were chattering excitedly. The adults were also having lively conversation and laughing. Grandpa seemed happy but he did not talk much. It was obvious however that Grandma was happy as she talked and laughed with the others. She loved it when her family came together.

Seun Alabi cut the birthday cake into small pieces, put them in a tray, and asked Mercy to take the tray around so everyone could take a piece.

At about six-forty, Papa's daughter, Stella, arrived, and apologized to her grandparents for coming late. She gave Grandpa a gift, and when she was ready to leave, Mercy went with her.

Lola asked some of her cousins to help tidy up and within minutes, everywhere was clean.

The event was one that everyone thoroughly enjoyed. Seun Alabi's immediate younger sister and her family were the last to leave at eight, and they offered to drop off the housekeeper at her house.

Lola eventually returned John's call at nine-fifty that evening. "I hope you're not sleeping already."

"No, I'm in my room watching TV." He took the TV remote, lowered the TV volume and leaned back against the pillows on his bed. "Were you in church?"

"No. Today is my grandfather's eightieth birthday." She said. She was lying in bed, physically exhausted but her heart was excited as she talked with John.

"Oh, wow! I wish him a very happy birthday and more years in good health, joy, and peace, in Jesus' name."

"Amen, thank you."

He spoke again, "The family must have had a big party for him,"

"No… no party."

He was surprised. "Why not?"

"He did not want a party."

"Oh, okay. Some people don't like parties, or noise actually," he said and chuckled, "but eighty is special. His children, or your grandma should have convinced him to do something."

"We did something. Family members and two of his friends came around, and my pastor was there to pray for him."

"Oh, good." He said. "Well, he must have had a happy birthday, and that was the most important thing."

Lola spoke again, "He did not want to celebrate it for a reason. Their first daughter died ten years ago, on December 26."

"Oh, I'm sorry to hear that."

"She passed on at the age of thirty seven,"

"Oh,"

"My mom was her immediate younger sister."

He exclaimed again and said sympathetically, "Her death must have hit the family hard."

"Yes, it did."

"What happened to her? Was she sick?" He wanted to know.

"Yes. Er- you know Mercy, Dayo's fiancé, right?"

"Yes, Dayo introduced her to me at the get-together."

"The woman was Mercy's mother."

"Oh," he processed the information and said, "Now I remember that you told me that you're Mercy's cousin… I see. Whoa! Mercy must have been young at the time."

"Yes, she was. I think she was around fourteen."

"Is she the first child?"

"Yes."

"What about their father?"

"That was what made the whole thing very sad. He had left his family before my aunt died, to start a family with another woman."

"Left his family- including the children?!"

"Yes, and he did not look back. He did not get in touch with anyone. My uncle had to take Mercy and her siblings in."

"That was really bad, but then, one should not be surprised- people who don't know God can do anything."

"That's the problem. He was a minister in his church. He was supposed to be born again."

"Hmm. Well, not everyone who goes to church knows God. If he truly knew God, he would not have left to start another family in the first place. That was wrong."

"He apparently did not think so. It was very recently that he got in touch with them."

"But if your aunt was thirty seven when she died ten years ago, and she was older than your mom, your mom must be young then."

She laughed, surprised that he was able to realize that fact so quickly.

"Yes, she is. She's forty five now."

"How old are you? Twenty nine or thirty?"

"Twenty nine."

"She must have had you at the age of-" he did a quick mental calculation, "sixteen?"

She laughed. "That's correct. She's Seun Alabi."

"Who is Seun Alabi?"

"My mom."

"Not Seun Alabi, the actress?!"

"Yes, she is." She laughed.

"What?! That Seun Alabi is your mom?" Seun Alabi was one of the biggest female actresses around.

"Yes."

He laughed. "Oh wow! This is interesting. She's one of my favorite Christian actresses. Whenever I see her face on the cover of any movie, I am certain that the movie would be good and well arranged. She's an incredible actress."

She was moved. "Thank you,"

"I've watched several movies she acted in. I've watched *Stranded, The Mighty One, Remember Me, Shattered Dreams.*"

As he mentioned some of the movies, she laughed.

"How come your last name is different?" He asked with interest.

"It's because she did not marry my father."

He suddenly remembered Seun Alabi revealing in one of the interviews she granted, which was on YouTube, that she was a single mother and had a daughter. *This is her daughter!*

"Oh, yes. I think that she mentioned something like that in an interview that I came across on YouTube." He said.

Lola knew the interview he was referring to—her mother had bared it all in the interview.

"She was one of those female students who followed male teachers about." Lola added.

He didn't remember hearing that in the interview, and he made a mental note to watch it again.

"She was impregnated by one of her male teachers?" He asked her directly.

"Umm hmm," she confirmed.

"Did he," he hesitated, then went on, "did he accept responsibility? I'm sorry to be asking so many questions, but I'm interested, you know, being a youth minister. Hope you don't mind?"

"No, it's okay." She said. "I sometimes refer to her case when counseling people or preaching. I've also talked about it a number of times to the teenagers I'm teaching."

He chuckled.

"My mom has revealed most of it publicly, anyway." She added.

"And you don't mind?"

"No, I don't. She talks about her life as a way of evangelizing, to make people know the difference that Jesus makes in a life. She made those mistakes before she knew Christ."

"That's right." He said and then added, "You're also free to ask me any question."

She chuckled. "I'll remember that."

"So, about your mom, did the man accept responsibility?"

"No. I didn't even know him until I was in University." She said without bitterness or anger.

"Whoa!" He exclaimed. "What brought you together?"

"He just suddenly contacted my mother." She said.

"Just like that?" He asked, surprised.
"Umm hmm."

CHAPTER 7

"So, how was growing up for you?" John asked Lola.

"My childhood was turbulent." She confessed. "My mom, being a teenager, had to go back to school. Besides, what did she know about parenting? She preferred hanging out with her friends and attending parties, to staying at home with me."

John laughed.

"So, my grandparents raised me. They had to do everything- bought toys for me, took me out with them, potty-trained me, registered me in school when I was old enough, and attended parents-teachers' meeting in my school."

"Wow!"

Lola went on. "Even though my grandparents loved me, I'm sure that having to take up the responsibility could not have been easy for them, it must have exhausted them in some ways."

"Hmm, I can imagine."

"It was also not easy for me. They tried to do their best, yet life was very tough, especially as I got older and realized that they were not my parents and my father did not want me. My friends had fathers, but I did not. My emotions became very unstable then." Lola confessed.

"I can imagine."

"I had peace and stability only when I became a Christian, which is why, whenever I have the chance, I now encourage young ladies to be careful."

"And how's your relationship with your mom?" He asked.

"It's okay, although when I was a teenager, before I became a Christian, I gave her a tough time. I saw her like a big sister who was trying to control me."

He laughed. "Were you calling her Mom, or some other name?"

"My grandparents made me call her Mom. They made me know that she is my mother; they did not pretend to be anything other than my grandparents. When I was much younger, there were times my grandparents forced her to take me to school. I didn't notice that anything was peculiar until when I was about age eleven and I realized that my friends' parents were much older. Whenever I told my friends that she was my mother, they would be like- *wha-t? Your mom is so young*! *How old is she*?"

He laughed.

"I began to feel embarrassed, and then the questions started rolling in—*who is my father? Where is my father? What exactly happened*? Several questions came to my mind."

He laughed again while she chuckled.

"My mom couldn't answer some of my questions, and in frustration, she would shout at me or beat me."

"Whoa! That must have been a tough time for you."

"It was." She admitted. "Everything is okay now, though, and we're having a great time together."

"Your grandparents must be wonderful people."

"They are. They were not Christians at the time, but they taught me a lot of things including the importance of hard work, the value of money, and how to save money."

"So, you and your mom live with your grandparents?"

"They live with us." She chuckled.

"Oh, I'm sorry,"

"We were staying with them in their rented apartment, and when my mom built her house, they moved in with us." She explained.

"I guess it's a case of all is well that ends well, then." He said.

"Yes, I guess. What about you? How old are you?"

"I'll be thirty one in August… August 27. When is your birthday?"

"April 24."

"You're turning thirty, right?"

"Yes."

"Wow! How are you celebrating it?"

She chuckled. "I'm not sure yet. I may just invite some few close friends and family to come around and have a form of fellowship, but definitely no party."

"Why not?"

"I'm not a party person. I don't want anything elaborate."

"I understand."

"What was your childhood like?" She asked, and he told her.

She asked about his arm, and he said that the bandage was removed the previous day.

They continued talking and it was ten minutes to midnight when they said goodnight and ended the call. Looking at the time on her phone, Lola smiled.

****

After the call, John went on YouTube, searched for Seun Alabi, and several videos came up. Most of them were the movies she featured in, both secular and Christian ones. He also saw four of her interviews, one of which he had watched before. He clicked on one of the other three and began to watch.

The host, a male, began by appreciating Seun Alabi for appearing on his show to be interviewed.

Host: Can you please introduce yourself to our audience?

Seun Alabi: I am Seun Alabi.

She went on to say a little about herself.

The host asked her about her educational background, and she answered, all the while, smiling.

As John looked at her face, he could see some definite resemblance between Lola and her mother.

The host asked further questions that made Seun Alabi reveal that she was not married, was a single mother, and had her daughter at the age of sixteen.

Host: Sixteen?

Seun Alabi: Yes.

Host: So, how did you feel when you discovered that you were pregnant? Were you scared?

Seun Alabi: (She laughed.) Definitely.

Host: So, what did you do? How did your parents find out about it, and how did they react?

Seun Alabi: Well, it did not occur to me that I could get pregnant, I was so foolish.

Host: (Laughed.)

Seun Alabi: And so, I was really scared when it happened. I didn't know what to do. I didn't think that I should tell the teacher that I was pregnant because he was preparing for his wedding at the time.

Host: Preparing for his wedding—and he impregnated one of his teenage students?! Whoa!

Seun Alabi nodded, and she could have said more to disgrace Lola's father but did not. The man might be watching the interview now, or come across it later, and saying bad things about him would not help her or Lola in any way. He definitely took advantage of her, but it wouldn't have been possible without her cooperation, she knew. She was the foolish one. Besides, she was now a Christian and she had forgiven him.

Seun Alabi: (She continued) And I couldn't tell my friends for fear of being exposed and ridiculed. For days, I thought about what to do. I couldn't sleep well, wasn't eating well, and couldn't concentrate in class. I eventually concluded that I would have to tell my parents, but how?"

Host: Did you at any time consider abortion?

Seun Alabi: Yes, it did cross my mind, but I was not sure how best to go about it. Besides, I was afraid that I might die, so I didn't take any step in that direction, and I'm glad that I did not. God blessed me with a wonderful daughter.

Host: So, what did you do?

Seun Alabi: I realized that I would have to talk to my mother, and with that decided, I began to plan and rehearse how to break the news to her. I chose a Saturday, and on that day, I woke up early. As I did my chores, I kept an eye on my parents, waiting for the time when my dad would leave the house for work. When he eventually did, I found that I couldn't go to my mom, I'd been paralyzed by fear.

Host: (Laughed)

Seun Alabi: (She laughed and continued) I stayed in the kitchen, thinking. I eventually summoned up enough courage and went to my mother and with my heart pounding in my chest, I told her that I was pregnant. Shocked, she screamed and started shouting at me, and as soon as my father returned home, she told him. They were both greatly upset, angry, and disappointed, but when they eventually got over the shock and calmed down, they supported me. They followed me to school to inform the school authority. I definitely wouldn't be where I am today without them. If they had reacted differently, or not supported me, only God knows what would have happened to me.

Host: How easy do you think it was for them to accept your situation?

Seun Alabi: It was definitely not easy for them. It was an unplanned responsibility as they had to take care of me and my baby. They also had to deal with people's comments and attitudes when it became known. It was definitely not easy for them and whenever I remember the past, I thank God for their lives, for not giving up on me and my child.

The host asked other questions which she answered, and they continued.

Host: You have been open about your faith. What made you become a Christian?
Seun Alabi: Like everyone who does not know God, I was lost in a world of sin, and I was miserable.
Host: What do you mean? After all, you were in the entertainment industry, doing what you loved to do.
Seun Alabi: Yes, I was doing what I loved to do, living my dreams, no doubt. Money was coming in, men were also coming, and I was having fun, but I knew that my life was empty. Deep down in my heart, I knew that something was missing, but I didn't know what it was or who could give me the answer. I also knew that I needed help, but I didn't know who to turn to, or trust. My mother had started attending a church, but I didn't trust pastors because of the many terrible things I'd heard about them. I eventually came across a pastor who seemed different. He began to tell me about God's love and as I listened to him, my heart began to open up. I eventually let God in, gave my life to Jesus and began to attend a Bible-believing church. That was how my life turned around.

Host: Interesting. Er- you left secular movies at the height of your career to focus on Christian movies. How has it been for you? Any regrets?

Seun Alabi: (She shook her head) No, none whatsoever. It's been wonderful.

Host: Is money still coming in?

Seun Alabi: (Laughed) It is a ministry for me; my calling. And a minister's priority should not be money. Pleasing God should be the focus, and God will provide and bless the person. So yeah, I'm blessed.

Host: Did you like acting when you were young?

Seun Alabi: Yes. In High School, I was a member of the school's drama group.

Host: And you eventually studied Theater Arts in the University.

Seun Alabi: (Nodded)

Host: Being a single mother, do you still hope to marry one day?

Seun Alabi: (Laughed) Well, er… I will marry if I meet the right man. Until then, I'll focus on what God has committed into my hands.

The host wanted to know if her daughter was also into acting, and she said no.

Host: Is your daughter married?

Seun Alabi: No, not yet.

John's mind went to Lola and he wondered if there was anything about her on YouTube. Without waiting to watch the interview to the end, he typed in Lola's name, but nothing came up.

He returned to the interview and watched it to the end, to see if Seun Alabi would say something that would be useful to him. As he watched her, he wondered what having her as a mother-in-law would be like, and he thought that it would be nice. She was definitely a Christian, a true child of God.

John's thoughts returned to Lola. From the little he had come to know about her, it seemed that she was very much involved in church, and he found himself wondering for the second time that day if getting involved with a woman who was a pastor was what he wanted. He thought about the challenges of ministry, and again, he told himself that if God was involved, he would marry her.

****

John called Lola again the next day and as they talked and laughed, she wondered if she had found her husband.

"So, when are you likely to come to Lagos?" She wanted to know.

"I hope that I'll be able to come at the end of the month."

That's two weeks away.

"I'll arrive on Friday evening, and leave on Sunday, immediately after church service."

Good. I'll be able to see him again.

"It's not very certain yet though." He added. "If this month end is not possible, I'll certainly come in February."

She decided to ask him, "I've been wanting to ask you, are you in a relationship? Is there a woman somewhere?"

He laughed. "No, I'm very much single."

"Were you in a relationship with a woman at any time?"

"Yes, but we had to end it."

"Why?" She asked.

"Ah, how do I explain it?"

She heard him sigh.

"I'll put it this way: her father was a serial cheat. He cheated on her mother several times—according to her."

"What's her name?"

"Lara." He answered.

"Okay, go on."

"That nasty experience affected her faith in men, and she found it difficult to believe that some Christian men would not cheat on their wives because they feared God. There was no trust in the relationship. If I did not answer her call on time, she would start asking me ridiculous questions, and saying some hurtful things." John said.

"She was a Christian, right?"

"Yes. I told her several times that I'm a true child of God, not at all like her father, but there was no change."

"Aww, she needed help. Did she go for counseling? Was she a member of your church?"

"No, she wasn't in my church." John answered. "She went for counseling once and was supposed to go back but she did not. She was a very private person."

"Thorough counseling and prayer would have helped her."

"Yes, but she must be ready to be helped."

"You could have stayed to help her."

"Yes, I could have stayed with her, to help her pull through but by then, I was already having doubts about the relationship." He said honestly.

"Hmm, I understand,"

"What about you?" John asked her.

"I was engaged to be married, but he died."

"I'm sorry to hear that." He said.

"Thank you."

"If it's something you can discuss, I'd like to know what happened. But if you don't feel like talking about it, it's fine, I'll definitely understand."

"He was on his way back from Kwara state when he ran into some armed robbers who robbed and shot him."

When she didn't continue, he asked, "When did it happen?"

"About four years ago."

"That's so sad." He said sympathetically.

They continued talking and when the call ended, she asked God, "Is he the one?"

She wasn't sure yet, and she didn't know him well enough to decide, but she was sure that she looked forward to his calls.

They talked every day of that week in the evening.

****

On Friday afternoon, John received a call to come for a job interview in Lagos on February 20, and when he called Lola in the evening, he told her about the call.

"Where is that?" She asked.

He told her the name of the organization and added, "It's not far from your office."

This seems to be getting better. "Yes. I know it's location."

"As it is, I think that I'll just wait till that time to come to Lagos." He said.

"Okay. Did you say February 20?" She looked at her table calendar.

"Yes."

"That's a Thursday." She said.

They talked for about half an hour.

On Saturday morning, one of the two men interested in the keyboard lessons paid for a month, and he and John agreed on when the lessons would start.

When John and Lola were talking in the evening and he told her that he had his first student, Lola wanted to know what he would do when he got a job in Lagos.

"There can't be a problem." He said. "The payment is monthly. I'll make sure that I do what I'm supposed to do before my relocation."

John and Lola kept in touch, and when he called her on February 13, he said, "I'll arrive on Wednesday evening, so I won't be able to see you on that day, but can I pick you up on Thursday evening for dinner if you're free?"

"I have service in church in the evening and I have to be there."

"Er… what time is it likely to end?" He wanted to know.

"Around eight-thirty.

"I'm not sure that will work."

"What time is the interview?" She asked.

"It's at one in the afternoon."

She did a quick thinking—she might have to take permission to close early on that day. She would need to meet with him so they could talk more and so she could know if God was indeed involved in what seemed to be developing between them.

"I will try to close early on that day so we can have lunch together afterwards." She suggested. "How does that sound to you?"

He liked the idea and told her so.

"Will you be going back that weekend?"

"Yes, I have to go back on Sunday." He answered. "Will I be able to see you again on that Saturday?"

She was happy to hear that, and she said yes.

After the call, John began to think of a restaurant he could take Lola to. It would have to be one that was decent, affordable, and served good meal, yet quiet so that they would be able to talk without any disturbance.

He had been praying about her. She was a good Christian woman, the kind of woman he'd like to marry and have children with. A woman he could talk to and share with.

CHAPTER 8

Lola considered letting her pastor know about John, and after service on Sunday, she went to his office.

"We haven't talked about relationship, but we've been talking regularly." She added. "I just thought that I should let you know."

The pastor asked some questions about John, prayed for her, and asked her to keep him informed.

At home in the evening, she phoned John. She was sitting in bed in her sleepwear, watching TV and eating popcorn. They talked for about an hour, and then said goodnight.

****

John waited for Lola to end the call, and then he put the phone down. He was lying on his back, in bed, and as he stared at the ceiling, thinking of her, his heart seemed to ache with what he had not said. After some minutes, he took his phone and sent a message to her.

Lola, I'm falling in love with you.

****

Lola's phone alerted her of a message and she took the phone. When she saw his name, she tapped on it to read, and what she saw made her smile broadly.

She wanted to reply that she loved him but stopped. No, she should wait until he came to Lagos and they'd talked more. They had become friends and she could discuss anything with him, but she still needed to be sure that he was God's will for her. She'd need to ask him some questions, to know more about him. She would also need to be sure that if they got married, he would support and encourage her ministry while he was also serving God in his calling.

She asked herself, *do I have too high standards*? She did not think so. All she wanted was a responsible godly man who would be capable of being her head.

She had to respond to his message however, and she was still staring at her phone and thinking of what to type when her phone began to ring.

She picked up immediately, "Hi, John,"

"Hi, Lola. You've read my message?"

She giggled, "Yes."

He was silent for some seconds and then he said, "I just wanted you to know."

"I appreciate that." She said, paused, and went on. "I'll want us to sit down and talk."

"We definitely will, when I come to Lagos."

There was silence for some seconds again.

Then he spoke again, "But do you feel anything for me?"

"Yes, I guess." She confessed.

"That's enough for me."

The way he said it made it seem like they had all the time in the world. Good.

****

John and Lola talked for some minutes more and when the call ended, John began to think of what he could buy for Lola from Akure. He did not think that it would be nice to see her in Lagos empty handed. He would have loved to buy her a beautiful top, but he didn't think that he should as he did not know her size. He thought of different things and eventually decided to buy some food items. Some women sold various food items at some villages, on the way to Lagos.

****

John and Lola talked on Monday and Tuesday, and on Wednesday morning when she was ready to leave the house for work, she sent a message to him, to wish him a safe journey.

He responded almost immediately, saying that he did not think he would be able to leave Akure before four in the afternoon because he had official meetings with some people.

Four in the afternoon?! Her mind flew to the past. The unfortunate incident that claimed Chege's life had happened around nine in the evening when he had almost reached Lagos. Some travelers who witnessed the attack rushed him to a hospital, but he could not be saved.

Concerned, she called John and told him, "Is that not rather late?"

"Not really. I should be in Lagos by eight if there's no traffic."

"But you know that there will be traffic," she argued.

He laughed a little, "I will be fine, God will protect me in Jesus' name."

"Amen, but—" she stopped. There should be no 'but' in this case, she counseled herself, after all, she was a pastor. She would have to put her trust in God, and deal with the fear that had reared its head.

She prayed for him instead, "Yes, the Lord will keep you safe in Jesus' name."

"Amen."

"But don't you think that you might be a little tired at that time? It's not a good idea to hit the road while feeling tired, you know."

When she realized that she had used the word 'but' again, she took a deep breath.

"I'll be fine." John said. "I intentionally went to bed early last night so I could have enough sleep."

She decided to let it go; she would pray instead. "Alright. Are you still at home?" She asked.

"Yes. I'm in the kitchen preparing my breakfast. I'd like to eat now because I may not have time to eat until after my meetings, and by then, there will be no time to sit down to eat a proper meal because I'll need to travel."

"But you will need to eat in the afternoon because of the long drive to Lagos."

"I will just get some snacks to eat."

"Okay. Try to leave Akure on time in the afternoon and drive safely please." She told him.

"I will, and I'll call you when I get to Lagos." He promised. "Thanks for your concern."

After the call, Lola took her car keys and left the house. On the way to work, she thought about how fear had almost gripped her when John said he would not be able to leave Akure before four. She definitely cared for him.

Rebuking the fear, she prayed that affliction would not rise again in her life, and that God would keep John safe.

At work, she asked her boss for permission to close at two in the afternoon of the next day, and it was granted.

****

John had packed an overnight bag for the trip to Lagos and when he was ready to go to work, he put it in the boot of the car.

It was indeed a busy day for him, but he was free to travel at about three-thirty in the afternoon. Getting behind the wheel of the Camry, he hooked the gray seatbelt, and turned on the CD player in the car to enjoy Christian music. On the way out of Akure town, he saw a middle-aged woman selling roasted plantain by the roadside. He slowed down, parked right in front of her, and looked at the plantains which were laid out on a wire gauze that was on top of hot charcoal.

"How much is that one?" He pointed at the one he liked.

The woman told him the price, and he bought three, along with roasted groundnut. Someone was selling soft drinks beside the woman, and he bought a can of coca cola and two bottles of cold water. He needed to keep hydrated. Putting the roasted plantain and groundnut on the front passenger seat, and the can of drink in the bottle holder beside him, he prayed, and as he pulled out back on the road, he reached out and took one plantain to eat.

As he drove on, on the highway, he was on the lookout for the people who sold foodstuffs along the road, and before long, he sighted them, on the outskirts of a village.

Good. Flickering on his signal light, he moved to the service lane, and slowed down until he reached the vendors. He stopped behind a car that had also parked to buy food items.

Some vendors immediately came to his car with their wares, and he bought lots of fresh corns, red bell pepper, onions, and habanero. He planned to give half of the items to Lola, and the remaining half would be for his family. He bought a large box from the vendors in which he put the ones for Lola's family, before driving off.

When he neared Lagos, he called Lola.

****

Lola had just returned from work and was in the kitchen to get her food.

"Where are you now?" She asked John.

He told her and added that he bought some items for her family.

"Are you back at home?"

"Yes, I got back not quite long." She said.

"Send your address to me so I can deliver the items to you."

"This evening?" She asked, surprised.

"Yes."

Oh, wow! She hadn't thought that she would see him this evening. Excited, she thanked him and said that she would send the address soon.

After the call, she considered the dress she wore- it was too casual. She would need to change into something better and get herself ready to meet him.

Bringing her food to the living room where her grandparents were seated watching TV, Lola sat down, and glanced at the clock on the wall. The time was seven-forty.

She forwarded her address to John, blessed her food and began to eat. She was still eating when her mother returned home.

Her grandparents were ready to pray with the family so they could go to bed, and the moment Lola finished eating, they prayed.

She took her plate to the kitchen, and back in the living room, her grandparents were getting up to go into their bedroom. She said goodnight to them and went to her room. There, she threw her closet open, considered the clothes inside, and chose to wear a mauve pink embroidered top on a long black skirt. She wore pink earrings and applied a little makeup to her face. She remained in her room and monitored her phone, so that she would not miss his call or message.

Shortly after, John called her again.

"Are you in Lagos now?" She wanted to know.

"Yes, and I'm on my way to your house."

"Okay, I'll be expecting you." She said. "Call me when you get here."

About fifteen minutes after, he called her again to say that he couldn't locate her house, and she gave him directions.

Few minutes after, he called to let her know that he had reached her house.

"Okay, I'm coming."

With her phone in her hand, she wore a pair of beautiful black slippers, and left her room.

Her mother was in the living room going through a movie script. She looked up and when she saw that Lola had changed her clothes, she asked if Lola was going out.

"No. A friend is here to give me something." Lola answered. "I'll be back soon."

She opened the front door and went out.

****

John got down from his car, and with a smile in place, he waited for Lola.

****

As Lola went outside to meet John, her heart was doing somersaults. She opened the gate of the house, stepped out, and saw him standing beside his car. The sleeves of the shirt he wore on jeans were rolled up.

When she got to him, he reached out and took one of her hands in his.

"It's good to see you again, Lola."

"Same here." She said, with a wide smile on her face. "How was the journey?"

He sighed. "It was okay."

"You must be tired."

"Oh, yeah, you can say that again."

Opening the boot of the car, he pointed at the box inside and told her the items in it. When he mentioned corn, she told him that her mother liked to eat corn a lot, and he smiled, happy.

"Thank you." She said.

Bringing out the box from the car, he followed her inside the house.

"Is your mom around?" He asked.

"Yes."

"Great! I'll get to meet her." He said, hoping not to seem starstruck when he saw her.

They laughed.

Lola opened the door of the living room, and her mother who was still in the living room was surprised to see a man. She had thought that the friend was a female. She put the papers in her hands down and looked at John as he put the box down on a side.

Lola introduced him, "Mom, this is my friend, John."

John greeted Seun Alabi respectfully. "I'm so glad and honored to meet you in person, Ma." Lola looked a great deal like her mother, he thought.

Lola's mom responded warmly.

"I'm one of your many fans. I've watched several of the Christian movies you acted in." He said pleasantly and mentioned five of the movies. "I celebrate God's grace upon your life, Ma."

"Thank you. God bless you."

"He brought this for us," Lola said and pointed at the box where it was. "Onion, pepper, and corn."

"Corn? That's my food." Lola's mom responded.

They all laughed.

"That's what I told him when he said he bought corn." Lola said.

John's smile was still in place.

Lola's mom thanked him.

"I want to see him off." Lola told her mother.

"Alright." Her mother said and then looked at John, "Nice meeting you."

"The pleasure is all mine, Ma." He responded politely.

He said goodnight to Seun Alabi and followed Lola out.

Outside, he asked Lola about her grandparents, and she said that they usually went to bed around eight.

"Does your mom know anything about me?"

"No, not really. I wanted us to discuss first," she answered, and then laughed, "but I'm sure she's waiting for me now with questions."

He laughed.

"What about you? Have you told your parents about me?" As she looked at him, she thought that he was the kind of man that many Christian women would find attractive.

"No, not yet, but I told my brothers."

She smiled. "Well, I've told my friend, Sarah, about you, and my pastor."

He chuckled. "Your pastor? What did he say?"

"He asked me some questions, prayed for me, and asked me to keep him informed."

He chuckled again.

They did not talk for some seconds, and then he said, "I always smile when I remember how we met."

"Me too. I almost did not attend the event, you know." She smiled and looked down.

"I almost did not attend too because of my arm. I came only because I did not want to disappoint Dayo. He wanted to hook me up with Mercy's friend, Lekan."

Surprise jerked her head up. "To meet Lekan?"

"Yes."

He told her about it.

Her eyebrows shot up as she said in an incredulous whisper, "Are you serious?!"

"Yes,"

"Lord, have mercy!" She exclaimed. "I had no idea! Mercy did not tell me, neither did Lekan. I will have to call Lekan."

"You can call her, but that has nothing to do with me."

"Oh, Lord!" She exclaimed again.

"Are you bothered?"

"Yes, somehow," she confessed. "We came together for the event."

"Yes, I know, but don't let it bother you in any way. I didn't make a promise to her, or show an interest in her. I didn't even exchange numbers with her."

"I understand, but ...it's just somehow. Mercy should have said something to me about it."

"She probably didn't say anything because there was nothing to say. I didn't make a promise to Dayo when he told me about Lekan."

She smiled. "It is well."

He raised his left hand and turned it to check his watch. "I will need to leave so I can get home on time and rest for tomorrow. Where should I pick you up tomorrow?"

They discussed how to meet the next day and which restaurant to go for lunch. Lola made him know that she planned to leave the office around twelve-thirty in the afternoon and would be at home by one-thirty.

"Alright. I'll pick you up. Two o'clock?"

"That sounds good." She confirmed.

They said goodnight and he got inside his car.

As he slammed the door and hooked his seatbelt, she stepped away from the car. With her arms folded across her chest, she watched him start the car, and as he drove away, he waved at her, and she waved back.

She walked through the pedestrian gate and as she locked it, she said *Oh God*! under her breath, still surprised about what she had just learned from him. *But why didn't Mercy tell me about the arrangement to hook him up with Lekan?*!

She walked slowly back into the house, and in the living room, Seun Alabi lowered the script papers in her hands. Smiling, she looked at Lola and asked who John was.

Lola giggled excitedly and sat down. "I told you that I exchanged phone numbers with a man at the get-together that Mercy invited me to in January."

"No, you did not,"

"I did, you must have forgotten." Lola said. "It was John, and we've been talking since then."

"He's a Christian, right?"

"Yes."

"Does he have a job?"

"Yes."

Seun Alabi wanted to know more about John, and Lola obliged.

"Do you love him?"

Lola nodded. "Yes, but I still need to get to know him better. I'm seeing him tomorrow so we can talk more. There are questions I need to ask him."

"Okay, but don't ask too many questions so as not to scare him away."

"Mom, I will ask him all the questions I need to ask him." Lola said firmly. "Yes, I'm trusting God for marriage, but what kind of marriage would that be if I wouldn't be able to ask him questions or if I overlooked some things just so he could marry me?"

Her mother took a deep breath.

Lola went on. "Mom, if he's the right man for me, he will stay irrespective of the number of questions I ask him. If he doesn't like a question, he is supposed to tell me, but if he runs away because of a question, then he's not worthy of me."

Her mother nodded. "You are right. Well, I will join you in prayers. God's purpose will prevail in Jesus' name."

"Amen."

Lola got up to check the contents of the box. "Hmm, lots of corn. Will you like to eat corn now so I can boil some for us?"

"Yes, please. Thank you."

Taking four corns, Lola went to the kitchen. She put water in a big pot, placed it on the gas cooker, and turned it on. Peeling the corns, she put them in the hot water, and covered the pot. Her mother did not like her corn boiled with salt.

She returned to the living room, sat down, and continued talking with her mother who was interested in knowing more about John.

After some minutes, Lola returned to the kitchen. The corns were ready, and putting them in two bowls, she brought them to the living room and set them on a table.

Her mother took one and started eating. "Hmm, very sweet."

Lola took her phone and began tapping on the screen.

Mercy, we need to talk. Call me ASAP.

She sent the chat to Mercy, but there was no response. *I will call her tomorrow*, she thought, and took a corn to eat.

When they finished eating the corns about half an hour after, Lola cleared the table and said goodnight to her mother.

In her room, she sent a message to John to thank him for the items, and he responded.

She sent another one.

Have you reached your house?

Yes.

Okay. Have a blessed night.

Thanks. You do the same. I'll see you tomorrow.

Her mind went to what he said about Lekan and she began to reflect on it. Hmm, there was indeed no reason for her to be bothered, after all, he did not make a promise to Lekan. He was not in a relationship with Lekan and so he was free to choose whomever he liked. But why didn't Mercy tell her?

Taking her phone, she put a call through to Sarah and told her about the situation.

"Have you asked Mercy?"

"No, I sent a chat to her but there's been no response. I guess she's not available. I'll call her tomorrow."

"Okay,"

"And I will call Lekan,"

"That's okay too, just to fulfill all righteousness, as the Bible says."

After the call, Lola began to think of the things she planned to discuss with John and how she would present them.

At work on Thursday morning, as she attended to different clients, counseling them on the banking products and services, she kept an eye on time, and at twelve-thirty in the afternoon, she carried her handbag and left the office.

CHAPTER 9

At home, Lola had a quick shower, and was on her way back to her room when John called her. He was through with the job interview and wanted to know if she was back at home.

"Yes. I'm almost ready. Call me when you get here." She told him.

She wore the gown she had chosen for the meeting, and by the time he called to announce his arrival, she was ready and looking beautiful.

John thought she looked elegant and told her so. "You look and smell great."

"Thank you." She said and smiled at him. He looked confident in the black jacket he wore over a white shirt and black trousers. "You look great too."

"Thank you." He responded and opened the front passenger door for her.

As she passed him, she could smell his cologne. *That's a good one.*

She entered the car, and he closed the door. Going to the driver's side, he climbed in and hooked his seatbelt. He started the car, inserted a CD in the CD player, and soon they were on the way to the restaurant with Ron Kenoly singing the worship song *Kabi O o si,* (Unquestionable) in the background.

"How did the interview go?" She asked, smiling at him.

"It went well, but I don't think that I'll take it. The salary is not good enough. I'll have to trust God for a better one."

She nodded in understanding. "God is able. What about the keyboard lessons? Is everything going on well?"

"Yes. A parent in my church wants his daughter to enroll, probably next week. They have a keyboard in their house."

They continued talking until they reached the restaurant. Inside the building, a male attendant in uniform approached them. Smiling, he welcomed them enthusiastically and asked if they'd prefer a table for two and when John said yes, he told them that he had one ready for them.

As he led them to the table which was in a corner, Lola admired the lovely décor of the restaurant.

They reached the table and as they sat down, the waiter asked if they'd had a good day, and they answered yes.

"Well, it's about to be better." He told them, still smiling.

"We sure hope so." John responded.

The waiter gave them two menus, left, but returned almost immediately with two glass cups of water.

John and Lola made their choices of food and drinks, and the young man left again.

"He's very friendly." Lola commented.

John agreed with a nod. "Yes, I like the chap."

"And this place is not bad,"

"No, it's not. I'm glad you like it." He said. "Er… let's pray."

He prayed briefly, thanking God for the moment, and Lola said *Amen*.

He asked about her day and while they were still making small talks, the waiter returned with their appetizer which was goatmeat peppersoup. Lola's drink was *zobo*, a tasty non-alcoholic drink, while John was served orange juice.

When the waiter left, Lola blessed all that she and John would eat and drink. Then, they took their spoons and as they began to take the soup, Lola made him know that there were some things she'd like them to discuss. John encouraged her to talk, and she began to ask the questions that were on her mind. As he responded, she looked at him closely, taking note of his facial expressions and body language.

The waiter returned, cleared the first course from their table and served the main dish, and after making sure that they had all that they wanted, he left.

Taking their cutleries, they continued talking as they began to eat the fried rice, plantain, and chicken which tasted as good as it looked.

Lola also wanted to know what John's purpose in life was, and he answered.

She could see that he had a natural reserve, but she did not feel that there was anything hidden about him. His answers pleased her, and she believed that he was not pretending.

Afterward, they talked about their feelings for each other, and then he proposed.

"I'm in this for marriage. I'd like to marry you." He said clearly, with a hopeful look.

And she said yes, elated.

"As I said yesterday, I've told my pastor, and he'd like to see you." She made him know.

"That's not a problem but can it be when next I come to Lagos? That should be next month. Will that be fine? I have to be at my office tomorrow, and I already have some commitments on Saturday. I won't be free until around four in the afternoon, but if you'd want us to go at that time, I'm okay with it."

"No, next month is okay." She said. "This Saturday is the fellowship for the girls, and it starts at four."

"Alright."

She wanted to know if he'd be able to attend the fellowship and teach, and he promised to be there.

They continued talking about their relationship, and he said he would inform his pastors in the two churches he attended, and they agreed to inform their families too.

"Are you going to inform your dad?"

"Yes, I will, at the right time. I'm sure he will be very happy." She said as she cut her chicken.

"When was the last time you heard from him?" He asked and carried his cup of juice to take a sip.

"He called me yesterday."

"Are you close to him?"

She shrugged. "Somehow. He's trying to bring me close."

They exchanged a smile.

She went on. "For example, he sent some money to me today."

"Oh, wow!"

She chuckled. "What I've noticed is that it's like he's trying to make up for the chaotic years. He goes out of his way to do things for me."

"Good."

"He even has a special name for me, he calls me Princess." She laughed a little.

"That's nice. Er- what's your middle name?"

"Omolola." She told him.

"Omolola Tolulope Thomas." He said thoughtfully. "Mine is Akinola."

She nodded. "Noted."

"What does your dad do?"

"He's a Professor in a University."

Her phone began to ring, and she looked at the screen. "It's my friend, Sarah. Excuse me."

He nodded and sat back.

"Sarah, hi – yes – yes, he's here. Hold on." She looked at John. "My friend will like to say hello to you."

"Is that the friend that you said you told about me?"

"Yes. She's my very good friend."

Smiling, he collected the phone. "Hello."

He exchanged greetings with Sarah, and then said, "I've told your friend that I'd like to marry her."

"Wow! And what did she say?"

"What did you say?" John asked Lola and gave the phone to her.

"I said yes." Lola said into the phone.

They all laughed.

"I'm happy to hear that." Sarah responded. "Lola, let's talk later, right?"

"Right." She said and returned the phone to John

"Hello,"

"It's nice speaking with you, John."

"Same here. I hope to meet you in person soon."

"You will, definitely."

He said goodbye, returned the phone to Lola, and Lola said goodbye to her friend and ended the call.

"She got married in December." She informed John.

"December? That's nice. Er, talking about marriage, when will you like us to get married, all things being equal?"

She smiled broadly. "I'll want it to be this year,"

He nodded, "I agree. We don't need a long courtship."

They were silent for some seconds, and then he added, "Marriage is one of the things that I asked God to do for me this year. Who would have thought that I would meet you at the get-together?"

She giggled.

"That reminds me, have you called Lekan?" He asked.

"No, not yet." Looking into her plate, she began to cut her chicken. "I'd like to talk to Mercy first before calling her, but Mercy did not respond to my chat last night. I'll definitely contact both of them today."

When they finished eating, they prayed—thanked God for bringing them together, and asked Him to perfect everything about them and their relationship.

Lola glanced at the time on her phone and said she'd need to leave soon. They had been there for almost three hours.

John summoned the waiter, paid, and they left. He drove her back to her house and left.

In the house, Lola changed into a more comfortable pair of shoes, told her grandparents that she was going to church, and left the house.

The housekeeper opened the gate, and as Lola drove out of the compound, she took her phone and called Mercy.

Mercy answered the call and after the greetings, Lola began, "When John came to my house yesterday evening,"

"John came to your house yesterday evening?"

"Yes,"

"Wow!"

They giggled.

She told Mercy what John said about Lekan. "Why didn't you mention it to me?"

"Well, initially, I thought it was not necessary, and later I forgot. I'm sorry." Mercy answered and said that Lola could call Lekan if she wanted to.

"Yes, I will."

When Lola told Mercy that she had lunch with John, Mercy wanted to know what they discussed, and Lola revealed that John proposed to her.

Lola added, "We will meet with our pastors and families soon and if everything goes right, we would love to be married this year."

"Everything will go right in Jesus' name." Mercy said and congratulated her.

When the call ended, Lola put her phone in the cup holder between the front seats and began to think of what exactly to say to Lekan. *Hmm, take control, Lord, in Jesus' name.*

She reached a traffic light and brought her car to a complete stop. Taking the phone, she opened her contacts, and scrolled to the *L*s. She searched for Lekan's name, and pressed.

As she waited for Lekan to answer the call, she wondered if Lekan was aware that she and John were communicating.

It was not answered, and she wondered if it was intentional. She was just thinking of calling again when her phone began to ring. It was Lekan and she answered it.

"Hello, Lola?"

"Lekan, how are you?"

"I'm doing well, thank you." Lekan responded. "And you?"

Lola answered that she was okay, and then said, "I've just heard about what happened at the get-together … I mean Dayo's arrangement for you and John to meet."

"There's no cause for alarm, Lola. Everything is fine."

Did I detect a tint of anger in her voice? Lola wondered as she went on, "I was surprised when John mentioned it in passing yesterday, I had to call Mercy to confirm."

"It's okay, Lola."

"Oh my God! I don't even know what to say,"

"There's nothing to say." Lekan responded nicely. "And er… actually, I've just arrived at a church for service. You should be able to hear some noise in the background."

"Yes, I can. In that case let me not delay you. I just thought that I should talk to you about the matter."

"Thank you. I appreciate it. Have a nice evening." Lekan told her.

When the call ended, Lola called John and told him of her conversations with Mercy and Lekan. They were still on the phone when she arrived at her destination.

"I'm in church now. I'll talk to you later." She told him.

She was in church for almost two hours and much later in her room, she called him and thanked him for the lunch.

"I should thank you."

The call lasted some minutes, and that night, she lay awake in bed for a long time, running all about her lunch with John through her mind- John's responses to her questions, his proposal, and all that they discussed.

It had been a wonderful moment and she had enjoyed herself. John had a good sense of humor and from the things he said, she could see that he truly loved the Lord, he was intelligent, and level-headed. He knew what he was doing. She could also see quiet self-confidence in him which she loved. She couldn't stand men who boast or try to be macho. He did not monopolize the conversation and when she talked, he listened.

He was also courteous, holding doors for her, and there was a way he looked at her that made her feel attractive. He was truly interested in her. *Thank You, Jesus.*

She smiled as she began to think of the kind of gown she'd like to wear for her wedding.

I hope his family likes me, and that our pastors approve the relationship. She would have to pray about these concerns.

****

In bed that night, John was thinking about Lola and his love for her when he suddenly felt inspired to write some poems about love. He got up, took his iPad, and began to type.

How beautiful you are, my dear,

Thirty minutes after, he was still typing on his device as words kept coming to his mind. He decided to use some Bible verses in the poems and opening his Bible to the book of Ecclesiastes, he searched for appropriate verses, and then wrote on.

He eventually stopped typing around two in the morning and as he held the iPad up, to read through what he had written, he decided that he would eventually turn this into a book, and dedicate it to Lola, after all, she was his inspiration. He hoped to show the poems to her one of these days, to get her opinion on what he had composed before sharing them with others. He would also have to think of how to make money from his poems. He decided to write as much as he could before leaving for Akure on Sunday.

Before sleeping, he sent a text to Lola to tell her he loved her. Knowing she would be sleeping at this time, he did not expect a reply, and there was none until three hours later.

****

On Friday evening, Lola visited Sarah at home. Sarah gave her food and as Lola ate, they talked and laughed.

Lola was on her way home at about nine that evening when John called to say hello to her.

“I’ll see you tomorrow afternoon at four.” He promised and said that he loved her.

That Saturday, he attended the fellowship. He was simply dressed—a plain black T-shirt on black jeans, and black snickers—and at the right time, he got up to talk to the sixteen girls in attendance about why suicide should not be an option for them at any time. As he spoke, Lola listened carefully and found that he did not just teach, he ministered. When he was through, some of the girls had questions which he answered, and then he prayed for them.

Afterward, Lola and John drove to a fast-food restaurant which was not far from Lola's house, and as they ate some snacks which included peppered snails, they enjoyed lively conversation. They talked about their love, family, the number of children they'd like to have, spiritual lives, jobs, and the fellowship for the girls. John also told her about the poems he wrote on Thursday night and his plans concerning them.

They spent about two hours and when the waiter brought the bill, she offered to pay.

"No. This is my idea, so it's my bill." He said. Bringing out his wallet, he extracted some money and settled the bill.

It had been a wonderful time, and when they eventually got up to leave, she asked him, "So, when are you likely to come down to Lagos again?"

"I hope to come in March, probably third weekend in March, and again in April for your birthday."

She was happy to know he had her birthday in mind. "I guess you will spend the Easter holiday in Akure."

"Oh, Easter, I've forgotten about that. I must be in Lagos for Easter as my church is having a special seminar."

"My church is also having a special seminar that I'd love to invite you to."

"No problem. We will work it out." He said, pleased at the chance to come to Lagos twice in April.

The next day, they went to their respective churches, and as soon as service ended in his church, John traveled back to Akure.

When Lola was eventually free, she called him to know if he had reached Akure, and he said that he was still on the way.

"Alright, take care of yourself, please."

At about six that evening, he called to let her know that he had reached his house.

The following weeks seemed to move at a snail's speed for Lola, but eventually it was the third weekend in March when John would be in Lagos.

That third Friday, he left Akure early for Lagos, and by four-thirty in the afternoon, he had reached his parents' house. He looked forward to the weekend and seeing Lola again.

When Lola closed at work, she went over, and he introduced her to his family.

In the afternoon of the next day, he came to her house to meet her family. Grandpa and Grandma were delighted to meet him.

Seun Alabi was happy to see him again and as she talked with John, Lola wondered how her mother would feel when she got married and left the house. Her mother would still have Grandpa and Grandma in the house, but it could not be for long. Seun Alabi was still young and beautiful. She was also a godly woman and Lola wished that her mother would find love and be married, instead of sitting by herself in the house. Lola decided to discuss with her mother later to know her thoughts.

Lola had fixed an appointment with her pastor, and at the right time, she and John left her house in his car for the church, to see her pastor.

The meeting lasted about an hour, and on their way back to her house to drop her off, he asked her, "What's your plan for your birthday?"

"As I told you the other time, it's going to be a quiet one. I will fast and pray on the day and break the fast around four in the afternoon, to accommodate whatever I'd like to do to celebrate."

"Good. We can go for dinner that evening."

"Okay. And after church service on Sunday, all roads will lead to my friend, Sarah's house for my birthday celebration."

"Sarah's house?"

"Yes, she and her husband offered to host it."

"Okay. Er … does that mean that your Saturday is free? Can we see my pastor, Pastor Dave?"

"No, it's not free. One of my cousins is getting married on that day,"

"That Saturday?"

"Yes, April 25." Lola confirmed. "I have to attend the church service and reception."

"Ok,"

"But we can see your pastor afterwards if he will be available. The wedding reception should be over by four."

"Alright. In that case, I'll contact him and fix a time." John said.

"Can you join me at the wedding reception that Saturday?"

"You'd want me to attend?"

Lola nodded. “Yes, if you can … and we'll see your pastor afterwards.”

He agreed. “I’d planned to see a friend, but I’d rather spend the time with you.”

She smiled. “Thank you.”

He wanted to know how many people might attend and when she said about twenty, he promised to bring a birthday cake and supply drinks for the event.

“Oh, thank you.” She told him.

They reached her house, she got down, and he left.

When her grandparents had gone into their room to sleep, Lola and Seun Alabi began to talk, starting with John’s visit.

Seun Alabi added, “I like him, I think that he knows what he’s doing.”

Lola smiled, happy. Then she said, “Mom, you will miss me when I get married, right?”

“Yes of course, but I’m glad that you’ll be getting married soon and starting your family.” Seun Alabi responded.

“I’ve been thinking about you, Mom,” Lola said quietly.

“Why?”

“You're still young and you’re beautiful. You still look great. I’d like you to be married too.”

Seun Alabi smiled. “If God makes it happen, I will. I think about it sometimes. It would be nice to be married and have a wonderful man I can call my own, but if it doesn’t happen, fine.”

“Yes but—”

“I’m not lonely, Lola. I enjoy my life. I’m busy with my work and service for God. I’m happy.” Seun Alabi said.

She added that being a single person, she could do whatever she wanted, go to church, sleep, go to movie locations, do whatever she wanted with her money, see friends, or just relax. She could decide to fast and pray for three days and not worry about cooking for anyone.

"Yes, but—"

"As I told you sometime ago, men still show interest in me, but I can't marry just any man. There are times that I miss having a man, but I'd rather wait for God than make another costly mistake. Not at my age, and not at my level as a Christian." Seun Alabi said firmly. "Marrying a wrong man could bring headache."

"With prayer, you will find the right man." Lola assured her mother.

"I know, but," Seun Alabi stopped and shrugged. "It's not a do or die thing for me, not anymore."

As Seun Alabi continued talking, Lola could see that her mother would love to be married. She also saw an emotion in her mother, but she was not certain if it was fear or sadness, or bitterness, or anger.

Lola decided to probe a little. "Mom, we don't usually talk about your love life, but now I'm interested."

Seun Alabi laughed.

"When was the last time you met a man who'd like to marry you?"

Seun Alabi laughed again, and then said, "Two years ago."

"Really? Wow!" Lola exclaimed. "He was a Christian, right?"

"Yes."

"So, what happened?"

Seun Alabi shrugged. "The truth is that I did not allow the relationship to grow."

Lola frowned a little. "Mom, why? You didn't like him, or what?"

"I liked him."

"Did you pray and thought that God was not involved?"

Seun Alabi did not talk for some seconds, and then, taking a deep breath, she said, "I don't think that I really prayed about him. Er… the truth is that I don't want to fall in love again … and before you say another *why*—"

Lola chuckled.

"I'll confess that—" she paused.

Lola waited.

"Well, maybe I'm afraid of falling in love again."

I see. Lola sat forward and asked quietly, "Why are you afraid, Mom?"

"All the times that I fell in love, they turned out to be disasters." Seun Alabi confessed.

She began to talk about her past relationships, starting from Lola's father, and the father of her second child who died. She also revealed that before she became a Christian, she was involved with a younger man who stole her heart, her dignity, her money, and her jewelries.

Lola's eyes popped up in surprise. "I didn't know about that."

"Yes, I know." Seun Alabi smiled. "It was a long time ago. Shortly after that, I became a Christian and decided to focus on my career."

Lola began to encourage her mother, adding firmly, "Don't give up on marriage!"

"I won't. It's just that in recent times, I – I don't know, but I'm afraid of taking a plunge."

"Fear is of the devil, Mom."

"I know."

"You can have it all, a successful career, ministry, and marriage. We will need to begin to pray about this. God is able to give you the right man." Lola assured her. "But you will need to deal with the fear, pray and rebuke it. Don't let satan stop you, Mom!"

"I won't." Seun Alabi said. "Don't worry about me though. When you get married and leave this house, I'll miss you, but I'll be fine. One thing I'm sure of is that God is with me, and He'll take good care of me whether I marry, or I don't."

Lola nodded slowly in agreement. "Well, I'll be praying for you, and when you meet the right man, I want you to know that you have my approval and support."

"I'll keep that in mind. Thank you."

Later in her room, Lola called John. They talked for some minutes and she prayed that he would have a safe journey back to Akure the next day. Afterward, she prayed for her mother.

After church the next day, Lola went to her father's house. She informed her father about John and promised to bring John to see him when next he came to Lagos.

John arrived for Easter celebration late on Thursday evening, April 9, by public bus. The special seminar in Lola's church was on Friday and he attended. Afterward, they visited Lola's fifty-six-year-old father who was happy to meet John.

Saturday was free for both of them as the program in his church would be on Sunday and Monday morning.

They decided to go to a beach that Saturday, and as they sat under a shed, watching the waves roll in and the people who were around, they talked quietly. He told her that he had fixed an appointment with his pastor, and that they would be seeing him after leaving Sarah's wedding reception. They both did not want long courtship and agreed to be married before the year ended. She mentioned that Mercy and Dayo would be getting married in October, and they fixed December for theirs, tentatively. Afterward, they prayed and spoke in tongues for about twenty minutes.

Lola worshipped in John's church on Sunday morning, and afterward, they came together to her house where he had lunch. He made her know that he would be returning to Akure the next day immediately after the seminar in his church, and would be back on Friday, April 24 for her birthday.

That Friday, Lola's birthday, she did not go to work as she had taken the day off. She fasted and prayed, and at about five in the evening, John arrived to take her out. She was touched that he had come to Lagos because of her.

He gave her two gifts, one was from him, and the other was from his parents.

"Dayo told me that he would be at the wedding reception tomorrow." He told her, on their way to a restaurant.

"Oh, that's good." She said.

Lola said she would pick John up the next day, Saturday, on her way to the wedding reception.

They continued talking, and eventually reached the restaurant where they had excellent meal and time together.

He shared the word of God with her and then prayed for her, asking God to enable her to live a life worthy of His call.

As he prayed, she said Amen.

"I pray He will give you the power to accomplish all the good things your faith prompts you to do, in Jesus' name."

"Amen!"

When they eventually got up to leave the restaurant, she told him, "Thank you for everything. I had a wonderful evening."

As she dressed up in the morning of the next day, Saturday, it occurred to her that Lekan would attend Stella's wedding ceremony, and she braced herself for the meeting.

When it was time to leave the house, she put her gift for Stella in her mother's car and entered her own car, while her grandparents joined her mother in her car, to attend Stella's church wedding service.

She soon reached her destination and as she drove inside the church compound, she saw Lekan and Mercy where they stood with the bridal train.

I knew it! She thought. She knew that Mercy was one of the bridesmaids, but she didn't know that Lekan was, too.

Parking her car, she got down, and went to greet the bride and her parents who were still inside the bridal car. Afterward, she went to Mercy and Lekan, and greeted them with a broad smile.

At the entrance of the church, an usher handed her a copy of the wedding program and led her to a seat. She sat down and glanced around—the hall was well decorated.

CHAPTER 10

At the right time, the congregation was asked to rise for the opening prayer by a pastor who went on to lead the prayer. This was followed by the processional hymn and soon, Stella entered the church hall on her father's arm.

It will soon be my turn to be married, Lola thought with a smile as she looked at Stella.

At about eleven-forty, she received a chat from John. He wanted to know where she was, and she replied that she was still in the church but the service would end soon.

Ok. I'll be expecting you.

When the service ended, Lola took pictures with the new couple and some family members, and then left. Inside her car, she called John to let him know she would soon be on her way to his house.

"Okay, I'm ready." He said.

She got to his house on time, but on the way to the reception, they ran into traffic. They continued talking and she told him about her meeting with Lekan. They also discussed her birthday celebration at Sarah's house that would hold the next day and John said he would be coming with his brother, Matthew.

The traffic eventually cleared and they had almost reached the venue when he received Dayo's call.

"Where are you? I've just reached the venue."

"We're almost there. We'll see you soon." John responded.

When the call ended, Lola asked him, "Are we joining Dayo and Mercy at their table?"

"Yes, I guess."

"Lekan will most likely be at the table with them." She pointed out.

He shrugged. "Okay."

"What will you do?"

"Do?" He looked at her briefly, "Nothing. I'll greet her, that's all."

They reached their destination, entered the hall, and saw that the newly wedded couple was already seated at the high table, flanked by their parents and some other people.

Glancing around, Lola saw her mother and her grandparents at a table, and she led John there to greet them. Her gift for the new couple was on the chair beside her mother.

"Will you like to join us at our table?" Seun Alabi asked her daughter, and then looked from her to John. She was obviously delighted that her daughter had found a good man to marry.

John smiled and looked at Lola.

Lola shook her head. "No, we will join Mercy at her table."

While Lola talked with her mother, John looked around, searching for Dayo and Mercy with his eyes, and eventually spotted them seated at a table.

When they left Seun Alabi's table, he told Lola that he had seen Mercy and Dayo and pointed at their table.

Lola saw that a lady was at the table with them, and she said, "Lekan's there."

"That's okay, but don't introduce me to her, and don't bring up the get-together issue." John told her. "We'll greet them, sit down, and enjoy ourselves."

Lola nodded. "I understand."

At the table, they greeted Dayo and Mercy, and then Lekan, before they sat down.

John sat next to Dayo, and Lola sat beside him. Only the seat next to Lekan's right was unoccupied.

Dayo and John began to talk.

Lola noticed that Lekan was using her phone, and she wondered if she was really busy on the phone or using the phone because she didn't want to talk to her and John.

After some time, Lekan got up and left.

Shortly after, Dayo said aloud to Mercy, "This is Victor coming with Lekan."

John and Lola looked in the direction and saw them.

Lola thought that they looked like a couple. *Is Lekan in a relationship? I didn't know that. Wow*! She smiled a little as she looked at Victor. Victor had short hair and short beard, was dark in complexion, and about five feet eleven inches tall.

When they reached the table, Dayo told Victor, "Good to see you. You didn't tell me you'd be coming."

"I know, right?" Victor said and laughed.

Mercy told Lekan, "I didn't know that you invited Victor."

Lekan simply smiled as she removed the gift item from the chair beside her.

Victor offered his hand in greeting to everyone.

As he and John shook hands, John looked at him closely and thought, *is this not the man who sat beside Lekan at the get-together*?

Victor sat beside Lekan.

Lekan wanted to know what Victor would like to eat, but he shook his head to decline.

"I don't want to eat now." He said. "Am I allowed to take it home?"

"Yes, but you can eat here, and I'll arrange the one you will take home."

"No, I'll just take it home. I try not to eat at parties."

Lekan smiled and said, "I understand, Pastor."

Is he a pastor? Lola wondered.

"What about something to drink?" Lekan asked Victor.

"Yes, please." He answered.

Lekan left and soon returned with a take-away bowl that contained food and two cans of soft drink which she placed in front of him.

The men were talking and laughing now.

A moment later, Dayo brought out his phone and took a picture of Mercy. He turned to John, held out his phone, and asked him to snap him and Mercy. John obliged.

When Dayo collected the phone back, he took a picture of Lola and John, and then Lekan and Victor.

Dayo began to press the handset and soon, John's phone beeped. As he took it to check, Lola heard Victor's phone sound too.

John saw the picture on his phone, smiled, and showed it to Lola. She liked it.

When Lola saw Victor show his phone to Lekan, she thought, *they are definitely in a relationship.* They also looked very much in love.

Some people began to share souvenirs to appreciate friends and families for taking out time to be a part of the celebration. Lola collected hers and got one for John.

Glancing around, she saw a woman who dumped the souvenirs she got inside a big bag that was under her table and then sat calmly like she had not received anything.

Lola was about to look away when she saw the woman take a bottle of non-alcoholic wine and three cans of soft drink from her table and put them inside her bag under the table. *That's wrong,* Lola thought and shook her head. *Some people are just greedy.*

About five minutes after, Lekan and Mercy left and soon returned, carrying three big plastic bags that contained well-packaged meat pies. Mercy gave two meat pies to each person at their table, before she and Lekan left to give meat pies to other guests at the reception.

That took about twenty minutes and when they returned, Victor announced that he would like to leave. Lola said that she and John would need to leave as well because of another appointment. Dayo too decided that he had spent enough time at the reception, and Mercy and Lekan got up to see the others off.

Outside, Lola and John said goodbyes to the others, and as soon as they were out of their friends' earshot, John asked Lola if Victor was Lekan's fiancé.

"I don't know, but it looks so." She said and laughed. "I will definitely ask Mercy later."

"Was Victor not at the get-together?

"At the January get-together?" Lola looked at him with a frown. "I don't know."

"I think that he's the guy who sat beside Lekan at the event."

Surprised, she asked him, "You think so?"

He nodded. "I'm not very sure but I think so. I recognize people easily. I'm good with faces."

"Wow! That's one area I'm not good at. I don't usually recognize people until about my fourth time of seeing them."

He chuckled. "I remember people's faces easily even if I've only met them briefly or seen them in passing."

"Wow!" She exclaimed, still looking surprised. "But how could you have recognized Victor? Did you talk to him at the get-together at all? I don't remember seeing you come to where we sat."

"No, I did not, but I was watching you from where I sat. I also looked at Lekan and the man she was talking with."

"I'll ask Mercy."

They got to Lola's car, entered, and headed for the church.

There, Pastor Dave was attending to someone, and they waited at the reception, but as soon as he was available, his secretary ushered John and Lola into his office.

"Good evening, sir." Lola greeted the pastor with reverence and awe. *This is Pastor Dave!*

He greeted them warmly and asked them to sit down.

He wanted to know a little about Lola, and she began to talk about herself, mentioning where she worked and how she was ordained a pastor. She did not forget to let him know that she was the evangelism leader of her campus fellowship in her final year in university, and she presently held a monthly discipleship program for some teenage girls in her neighborhood.

"Good." The pastor said, when she stopped. "It's good to know that you're living for God. Now, concerning marriage, the Bible makes us know that marriage is a great thing because God established it. It was God's idea, not anyone else's idea. The Bible also reveals that a man who finds a wife finds a good thing and obtains the Lord's favor."

As he spoke, he looked from John to Lola. And then, resting his gaze on John, he added, "So, if you have found the woman you'd like to marry, I'm happy for you. However, it's important to get it right from the beginning, do you understand?" He shifted his gaze to Lola.

They answered *yes sir.*

The pastor went on. "Aside being in love with each other and praying to know the will of God, a couple in a relationship must also count the cost. There are things they must consider and questions they should find answers to before marriage, to be sure that all is well."

Looking at John, he said, "You have heard us preach about all these things in church, and you understand what I'm saying, don't you?"

"Yes, I do, sir." John answered.

"And you must have heard these things in your church too." He said to Lola.

"Yes sir."

As John and Lola listened to the pastor, they couldn't help wondering where this would lead. Had the Holy Spirit told him something?

"She's a pastor, you're not a pastor … or maybe I should say that you're not yet a pastor because God can move in your life at anytime. So, one of the questions you will need to discuss is - what if she feels led by God to start a church, or if the church asks her to head a parish? Have you thought about it?" He asked John, and then looked from him to Lola, and back to him. "Have you thought about it? Can you cope?"

John took a deep breath.

Pastor Dave spoke again. "What if for some reasons she tells you that she'd like to be in full-time ministry and she resigns from her banking job? These are just some of the questions to settle in your heart and between yourselves, to be sure that you're compatible and ready for marriage. Okay?"

They said *yes sir.*

Looking at John, the pastor went on, "Do you also realize that if God does not call you to be a pastor, there will be times that you'll be standing together and someone will address her as Pastor, and you as Brother,"

Hmm, that's true, John thought.

"How would that make you feel?" The pastor asked. "You may be wondering why I'm saying these things … I'm saying them to make you think, talk, and pray. They may seem like nothing but if a couple is not well prepared, they could be thrown off balance, especially the husband."

Hmm.

Pastor Dave continued. "A man may begin to compete with his wife, feel threatened in some ways, or begin to complain. There would be times she would come home tired and drained, unable to cook right away."

John took a deep breath.

"Also, I'm sure you know that being in ministry will involve sacrifice, and by that I mean the things you will need to give up in order to please God—the sacrifice of your time, comfort, even money, as necessary. There will be times when she may need to be in church; there may be an event or a meeting after church service which she must attend. There will be times you'll be at home alone with the children. Sometimes, there would be a reversal of roles. Have you thought of these?"

Lola and John didn't talk as they continued looking at him.

"A reversal of roles, sometimes, and not all the time." The pastor said and raised his right index finger for emphasis. "And it should not be often because the family comes first and the woman has a role to play in the home; she remains a wife and a homemaker. Do you understand, Lola?"

"Yes sir." Lola answered.

The pastor looked from Lola to John. "I need to also say that being a pastor does not make her in any way the head of the home, or your head. Being a pastor is a calling to serve God and His people; it's a divine purpose, but when you get married, she becomes your wife and you become the head. At home, she's fully your wife, and you are the head of your home. You should lead prayers in your home and give direction to the family as the Holy Spirit leads you."

John and Lola nodded in agreement. They were glad that they were hearing these things.

"I'm just asking you these questions. There doesn't have to be any problem, and there won't be any problem if both of you submit to God and have a good understanding of what marriage is all about." The pastor added.

John nodded.

Looking at John, he said, "For you, if you remain a committed Christian and intimate with the Holy Spirit, you will be fine. The Holy Spirit will teach you all things. Attend services, be a good Christian, support your spouse, pray for her, be a good head and leader to her, and be united with her."

"Yes sir."

He continued, still looking at John, "Let me also say that being a pastor does not mean that she will be perfect. You are also not perfect but as both of you walk with God you will learn and grow, and tend towards perfection."

"Yes sir."

"Also, you don't have to be an ordained pastor, and don't try to be one. Don't compete with her. Don't be embarrassed when people address her as Pastor and call you Brother. And don't let anyone tell you that you are the man and should be the pastor. It is God Who calls. Don't step into a calling that's not for you. Don't try to have a calling like hers. Do you understand?"

"Yes sir."

"You have your own calling, stay in it, but if God leads you in the direction later, so be it." The pastor said. "Of course, if a spouse is called, the whole family is called in one way or the other. Aaron's family in the Bible is an example. And so, the husband, wife, and children should not be passive."

"Yes sir."

The pastor went on. "There was a time that churches did not ordain women, but more and more women are getting involved now in ministry. And so, when she is leading in church, you may need to take a backseat. But don't let it bother you, you're still her husband and her head. Both of you must not forget that!" He looked at Lola.

"Yes sir." She responded.

"Also, when you're in church, or you're talking about her to a church member, you will need to address her as pastor."

John nodded in understanding.

Pastor Dave told Lola she must submit to John in marriage, in accordance with God's word. He added, "In marriage, you should create time for your family- your husband and children. Your family matters, so, don't neglect it. Don't let ministry or whatever you think that God is asking you to do tear you apart, God is not an Author of confusion."

Lola nodded and said *yes sir.*

"If there's anything you can't handle, discuss, and pray. If you still can't handle it, then don't hesitate to see me and my wife." He looked from Lola to John.

John said *yes sir.*

Pastor Dave talked some more and then said, "Simply put—in marriage, focus on your blessings, your love, and God. And follow marriage principles."

"Yes sir."

"I don't think that I need to tell you to stay away from sexual sins."

"No sir," John responded.

He looked at John. "You are a worker in this church and she's a worker in her church. She's not just a worker, she's an ordained pastor. Everyone who names the name of the Lord must depart from iniquity."

"Yes sir."

"Good. Er, when do you hope to get married? I wouldn't advise a long courtship."

"Yes sir. We are looking at December." John responded.

Pastor Dave nodded. "December is okay. You will need to inform the church on time to secure the date and ensure there is no conflict with other church events. You will also need to see the marriage committee of the church, headed by my wife, for premarital counseling."

John said he would.

"When you get married, she will join you in this church, right?"

"Yes sir." John answered and looked at Lola.

She nodded. "Yes sir."

"Good. My wife holds a quarterly program for female pastors and ministers. I'd like to encourage you to be involved. You'd be greatly blessed." The pastor told Lola.

Afterward, he prayed for John and Lola, they appreciated his counsel, and left the church.

When they neared Lola's car, John said, "I'll drive."

Lola brought out her bunch of keys from her handbag and gave it to him.

On the way to John's house to drop him off, they began to discuss some of the things the pastor had told them.

Then John said, "I'd be proud to be a pastor's husband."

"And I'd be proud to be Brother John's wife." Lola was obviously excited about the life they would share.

They laughed.

"Who knows, you may become a pastor in future." She added.

"If it's God's will." He said and shrugged. "Until then, I'll continue in my calling, ministering to teenagers and my family, including my *pastor wife*."

"I'll be a good wife to you by God's grace." She promised.

"About sex, we will wait until we're married. We're Christians and we must please God."

"Yes." She nodded.

They continued talking and agreed on the strategies to put in place to guard against premarital sex.

When they reached his house, he stopped the car, but did not get down.

He chuckled and said, "I have kept myself; I've never done it."

She looked at him. "Sex?"

"Yes."

"Really? Wow!" She exclaimed. How she wished that she could say the same thing about herself. She used to say it when she was in university, to encourage the ladies around her, especially during counseling, or Christian Sisters' Day. How could she have destroyed her testimony?

She wondered. Whenever she remembered the past, she was filled with regret. The pressure from Chege was too much for her to handle, but she realized now that she should have ended the relationship with him. Even if a man would marry her, she was not supposed to have sex with him before marriage, being a Christian.

"I've been keeping myself." John added and smiled. "And that's what I'm teaching and encouraging the teenagers to do."

"Wow! That's great. That's how it's supposed to be." She said and looked away.

Should I tell him about myself, or wait for him to ask? If he doesn't ask, should I keep quiet about it? Doing a quick thinking, she told herself that the right thing would be for her to talk now. Telling him on time was the best way of dealing with the issue. Even if she did not talk now, the truth would come out at a point, or on their wedding night.

But will he still want to marry me after my confession? She wondered. Well, she would have to do the right thing and trust God to work things out, she decided. God would not bring her this far to let her down, she believed.

She was still thinking of how to start what she had to say when he spoke.

"What about you?"

She took a deep breath, exhaled slowly and began, "I was keeping myself. It meant so much to me, but Chege wanted sex and … I eventually let my guards down, unfortunately."

He did not talk as he continued looking at her.

Knowing he expected her to say more, she did without looking at him. "He said that God would forgive us."

"He said that?"

She nodded, filled with regret.

John looked angry. "The man was not a good Christian; he was a destiny destroyer. I thought that you said he was a pastor."

Lola nodded again.

"You were not the only lady he was sleeping with, most likely, and he must have told them the same thing he told you." He added with a grimace.

"It was a possibility." She admitted.

He made a sound.

That made her look at him and she said, "I'm sorry,"

"It's okay." He said gently. "You have asked God for forgiveness, right?"

"Yes. After Chege's death, I had to rededicate my life to God. I didn't want to go into sin, but Chege wore my defenses down." She stopped and sighed. "I have no excuse, anyway."

Taking his hand, she apologized again for not keeping her body for him.

He turned his hand so that he was the one holding her hand. "Was there any other man after him?"

She shook her head. "No."

"Well, all that is in the past. We will focus on God and build a good future together."

They talked a little more before he alighted from the car. She got in the driver's seat, and he waved as she drove away.

****

In his room later, John thought about Lola's confession. He had been hoping to marry a virgin, having kept himself too, and he had been certain that she would be a virgin, being a pastor, but now that she had confessed that she was not, what should he do?

He remembered his words to her in the car—*all that is in the past. We will focus on God and build a good future together*. Was that the right thing to say? Did he make the right decision? Hmm.

What scriptures supported this decision of his? As he thought about this, some Bible verses came to his mind, including Proverbs 28:13.

People who conceal their sins will not prosper, but if they confess and turn from them, they will receive mercy.

Proverbs 28:13 NLT

Taking a deep breath, he began to consider their relationship. He also thought about their discussion in her car and how she had apologized twice to him for not keeping her body for him. What if she had withheld the information from him and lied about her status?

He eventually concluded that the important thing was who she was now, and he believed that she was a committed Christian. Besides, she would have forgiven him if he was the one who had not kept himself. He must do the same. He loved her anyway, and what happened was in her past.

Now, he had his answer. Focusing on God was what he would do, he would not focus on the past. He prayed and asked God to help him focus on the right things.

Afterward, he called Lola.

****

On the way home, Lola was running their conversation through her mind. John had not condemned her, but she had seen something that looked like disappointment in his eyes. And when he was alighting from her car, he had not said he loved her as he usually did since the beginning of their relationship.

Everything had been going on well, why did it have to end this way? She thought.

Help me! She cried out to God. *Why didn't I keep myself? Why did I allow myself to be deceived by satan and Chege?!*

At home, her mother and grandparents were not back, and she went straight into her room. Changing her clothes, she knelt on the floor and rested her head on the bed.

She did not regret her confession to John because she did the right thing, but what should she do now? Should she call John? He had said that they should focus on God and the future but did he mean it?

She began to ask God for divine intervention and wisdom to handle the matter.

Her phone suddenly began to ring, and she looked at it. It was her mother, and she answered it. Her mother wanted to know where she was, and she said she was back at home.

"Okay, we're almost at home. I have some things in the car and will need your assistance please." Her mother said. "I'll call you when we arrive so you can come out."

"Okay, Mom." Lola said and looked at the time on her phone, it was eight-twenty.

Some minutes after, she received her mother's call, and she went outside.

At about nine, she was back in her room, and getting in bed, she lay on her back and continued praying. She decided that she would not bring up the matter unless she had a reason to.

Some minutes into the prayer, her phone began to ring again and when she saw John's name, she quickly answered it. He just wanted to know when she would likely get to Sarah's house, and she told him.

She expected that he would talk about what they had been discussing in her car, but he did not, which made her feel uncomfortable. *Maybe I should say something.*

But before she could, she heard him say *I love you*, and she said the same words to him.

When she heard him say *As I said in the car, we will focus on God, His words, and our love,* her fears evaporated.

After church service on Sunday afternoon, some of Lola's friends and cousins met at Sarah's house to celebrate Lola's birthday. John and his brother arrived with a cake and four of 24-count cans of soft drinks. About thirty people attended the event including Mercy and Dayo. Everyone had plenty to eat and drink, and everything went well.

Before John and Lola left the place, they talked, and he assured her of his commitment to her.

At home later that Sunday evening, Lola called Mercy and after thanking Mercy for her gift and attending her birthday celebration, she asked, "Was Victor at the get-together in Dayo's house?"

Mercy burst out laughing. "Yes."

"Really?" Lola exclaimed. "I didn't recognize him; it was John who did. Wow! He and Lekan are in a relationship, right?"

"Yes." Mercy confirmed to her, laughing again. "He proposed to her yesterday, right at the car park of the reception venue."

Lola exclaimed again, and then asked if Victor was a pastor and Mercy said yes.

Mercy added, "I don't know if he's been ordained though. His father is the pastor of *Grace and Glory Chapel* -"

"*Grace and Glory Chapel*?!"

"Yes. Have you heard of the church?"

"Yes. One of my colleagues attend the church." Lola said.

"Victor's also a medical doctor,"

Another surprise. "A medical doctor?!"

"Yes."

"Wow, I'm happy for Lekan, that's awesome!" Lola said. "Can I call her to congratulate her?"

"Yes, you can."

"If she wants to know how I got to know, I will have to mention your name. Is that okay?"

"Yes, sure, but their relationship seemed pretty obvious yesterday at the table."

Lola laughed. "Yes."

After the call, Lola thought about Lekan and Victor, and smiled.

She was a pastor and would have loved to marry a pastor, but God chose to bring John to her, and led Victor who was a pastor and a medical doctor, to Lekan. *Hmm.*

Indeed, God's ways are not our ways. God knows what He's doing however, and knows the end right from the beginning, she thought.

Well, if God gave her John, then John was the right man for her. She loved John already anyway, and he loved her.

It occurred to her that if Victor had shown an interest in her at the get-together, she would not have responded well because she would have thought that he was younger than her. Even though she knew that it was not wrong to marry a younger man, she did not want it. John was older than her which was an answer to one of her prayers.

She smiled again. God had actually given her the right man. John might not be a pastor, but he was a good Christian, and would be a good head in marriage.

Deciding to pray, she thanked God for bringing John into her life, and prayed that God would lift him up and bless their union.

Afterward, she called John and told him what Mercy said about Lekan and Victor.

"Well, I guess it's a matter of *all is well that ends well.*" He said.

They laughed.

They continued talking, and he told her that he would be leaving for Akure very early on Monday morning.

After the call, Lola put a call through to Lekan.

CHAPTER 11

Three weeks after, John called Lola and told her that he would be having a job interview on phone on May 26.

He added, "It's an international company and the person who linked me said that the pay is good."

The name of the courier service company was *Ferries International,* and they agreed in prayer that the interview would be successful.

Afterward, he did some research on the company, and began to prepare himself for the interview.

On the day, he put a copy of his resume and a list of the questions he would like to ask by his phone. At the appointed time, the call came in and he picked up.

The interview lasted about half an hour, and immediately after, he called Lola to let her know that it went well and what the salary would be if he got the job. The salary would be thrice what he was being paid now.

"Is that the only interview, or will there be another one?" Lola asked.

"No, I think that's all." He said. "The manager, Bori, said that he will contact me before the week ends to let me know their decision."

"It will favor you, we have prayed about it," she assured him. "You will get the job in Jesus' name."

"Amen. I believe."

The next day, he told her that he got the job.

Thank You, Jesus! Lola was happy. "When are you expected to start?"

John explained that he would start working at the place on the first of July and would give a month's notice at his present place of work.

He added, "I won't be able to come to Lagos until then because I have a lot of things to tidy up at work. I will also have to give enough keyboard lessons to my students to cover their payment for the month."

"Okay. What do you think about us handling the fellowship together when you're back in Lagos?" She asked. "We can invite teenage boys too."

"Awesome!" He said, sounding intrigued by the idea. "I think we should also pray about making it a weekly event."

Lola liked the suggestion.

While John was praying later, his mind went to his list at the beginning of the year, and he smiled. He had a good job now, he had an additional stream of income, he had found his bride, and the youth ministry was about to take a new shape. God had answered all his prayers.

Thank You, Jesus!

****

That Wednesday evening, Mercy called Lola to let her know that the second week of October had been fixed for her wedding. The traditional engagement ceremony would hold on Friday evening, to be followed by church service on Saturday morning.

Lola congratulated and informed Mercy about her own plans.

"John and I are looking at December, most likely the first Saturday. He just got a new job, and he will be moving back to Lagos."

"That's awesome!"

Lola wanted to know how Lekan and Victor were doing, and Mercy said that the couple had decided to get married next year.

"I almost can't believe that Lekan and I found our men at the get-together in January."

Mercy laughed.

"Whenever I think about how everything has turned out, I still feel amazed."

"I know, right?" Mercy said. "Dayo and I are also very happy for you. God is the perfect matchmaker."

Lola agreed, and then asked Mercy what she would want her to do at her wedding.

****

John gave a month's notice at work and informed the people he needed to inform. His colleague in Akure was thrilled for him but sad that he would be leaving. He had enjoyed working and sharing an apartment with John. He wished John well and on John's last official day of work, some of their friends and neighbors were invited to the house for dinner, to give John a rousing send-off.

John returned to Lagos on Monday, June 29, and resumed at *Ferries* on July 1.

When he and Lola were talking later that day in the evening, he told Lola that the quarterly event for female pastors and ministers by his pastor's wife would be coming up soon, and Lola said she'd like to attend.

"I'll get the details for you." He promised.

About two hours after, he forwarded the details to her on WhatsApp. The theme was AN EXEMPLARY LEADER, and it would hold in the church hall on the third Saturday of July.

****

On that third Saturday, Lola went to *Great Grace Chapel* for the event. It started promptly and at the appropriate time, the pastor's wife, Pastor Teni, came to the podium. She welcomed everyone to the event and then recognized the new-comers. Lola was among those who stood, and they were led to a side in front, to sit.

After a few announcements and some songs to worship God, it was time to minister, and Pastor Teni prayed. She began to talk and the first scripture she read was John 15:16.

"You did not choose Me, but I chose you and appointed you that you should go and bear fruit, and that your fruit should remain, that whatever you ask the Father in My name He may give you."

Looking up from her Bible at the audience, she said, "As a female pastor, or a woman in ministry, you need to keep this verse in mind and have a deep understanding of it. This is because what Jesus said to His disciples applies to you. What God says to one, He says to all."

She paused for a few seconds to get their attention. Then she spoke again. "Jesus said to them, "YOU DID NOT CHOOSE ME! I CHOSE YOU!"

She paused again before she went on, "Though a woman, I'VE CHOSEN YOU!"

She stopped and laughed a little. "Glory to God!"

Some of the women clapped while some shouted Hallelujah!

She continued, "Don't let anyone despise you, look down on you, or tell you that you don't qualify to be a leader in the body of Christ because you're a woman. You did not call yourself, GOD CALLED YOU!"

Some people stood and clapped.

"If they have any problem with it, they should ask Jesus."

The pastor talked about this for some minutes before going on to talk about Jesus' expectations of everyone chosen and called into ministry—to go and produce lasting fruit.

And then, she began to talk about what it means to be an exemplary leader. She added, "There's a book written by a woman—Pastor Taiwo Iredele Odubiyi—for women in ministry."

She held up a copy of the book. "The title is *God's Words to Women in Ministry*, and my husband, Pastor Dave has asked me to give a copy to every woman present."

Everyone clapped.

Opening the book, she said, "I'm going to read a portion of it."

As a woman in ministry, you should be an example in your words, conduct, love for people, faith in God, and moral purity.

You should also learn to apologize when wrong. Don't be proud, be honest, be truthful, faithful, dependable, a promise keeper, and a good follower of the Lord Jesus.

Also, in ministry, show seriousness and an excellent spirit.

And in all things show yourself to be an example of good works, with purity in doctrine [having the strictest regard for integrity and truth], dignified, sound and beyond reproach in instruction, so that the opponent [of the faith] will be shamed, having nothing bad to say about us. (Titus 2:7-8 AMP)

As the woman continued preaching, Lola listened intently. She had been concerned about leaving her church for another church, but now, she felt happy, and looked forward to what God might have in store for her in this church where John worshipped.

****

Lola and John talked on phone and met regularly to discuss and plan their future. John would rent a two-bedroom apartment in September, their engagement ceremony would hold on the first Thursday in December while the church wedding would hold two days after, the first Saturday of the month of December, in Lola's church. They planned to travel to Dubai for their honeymoon.

They also arranged for their parents to meet, and John's elder brother promised to attend the wedding with his family.

****

Mercy and Dayo got married in October. Lekan was the best lady while Victor and John were among the groomsmen. As the officiating pastor joined the couple in holy matrimony, Lola watched with interest. *I'm the next person to get married in the family. How amazing is that!*

She had kept in touch with Lekan and when the ceremony ended, she went to Lekan to invite her and Victor to her wedding.

"The traditional engagement ceremony will hold on Thursday, December 3 while the church wedding and reception will hold on Saturday, December 5. Kindly honor us with your presence."

Lekan congratulated her and prayed that Lola and John would have a wonderful life together. She promised to be there. "If Victor is available, we'll come together."

"Thank you. I'll get the invitation card across to you as soon as it's available." Lola promised.

That first Thursday of December was a wonderful day for the parents of Lola and John as they hosted the traditional wedding ceremony of their children at *Glorious Affairs Event Centre*. Lola and John dazzled in their turquoise and yellow attires with matching accessories. The coral beaded jewelry worn by Lola which hung beautifully on her neck was made by Mercy.

Lola's friends who looked gorgeous in red and black attire moved around to ensure that everything was fine.

Some actors and actresses stormed the event to support Seun Alabi, and it was obvious that they were having fun as they laughed a lot. Seun Alabi also exuded so much joy. A host of press and photographers were also present to cover the colorful ceremony, while some individuals used their cellphones to record and take pictures. The lively event which kicked off at around three in the afternoon with prayers, lasted about four hours.

On Saturday morning, Lola woke up early, both excited and filled with anticipation. After praising God and committing the day into God's hands, she got up from bed. Her best lady, a minister in the church, was with her. In the house were also two of her friends, three cousins, and her bridal train.

After a light breakfast, everyone began to dress up and soon, they were ready. Lola posed for some photographs before heading outside with her bridal train.

Her grandparents and some people entered Lola's car, while Seun Alabi and the best lady joined Lola in the well-decorated Mercedes Benz car that would take her to church. The car and driver were sent by a friend of Seun Alabi for the purpose of the occasion. When it was time, the vehicles in front of the house left in a convoy, following the bridal car to the church.

They got to the church around nine-thirty eight, and some people came over to congratulate Lola and her mother who were still inside the air-conditioned bridal car.

Lola could see the decorated car that brought John where it was parked. There was no one inside it as John, the best man, and the groomsmen which included Dayo, had already gone inside the church hall to occupy their seats, ready for the service that would begin at ten.

Glancing around, Lola couldn't see her father, his car, or his wife. Her father was supposed to meet them in church.

"I can't see Daddy. Is he here yet?" She said aloud.

"Why don't you call him?" Seun Alabi responded as she prepared to alight from the car. She looked amazing in the custard yellow traditional attire with matching accessories that she wore.

Lola's best lady had Lola's cellphone and Lola was about to collect it when she saw her father's car arriving.

"He is here." She said, feeling relieved.

The driver of the car parked, and Lola's father and his wife who wore blue attires alighted from the backseat.

They came over to the car and after greeting everyone, his wife entered the hall.

Lola's mother got down from the car, greeted some guests in the compound, and went inside the hall.

"Dad, why don't you come and sit down?" Lola told her father who was standing close by.

He checked his watch and declined. "There's no need. It's almost ten."

Lola waited in the car until it would be time to walk down the aisle on her father's arm.

Just then, Sarah and her husband arrived, and her husband congratulated Lola before going inside the church. Heavily pregnant Sarah opened the front passenger door and settled uncomfortably into the front seat. She prayed for Lola before they started talking and laughing.

A photographer was nearby, taking Lola's pictures with the different people who came to congratulate her.

At exactly ten, the ceremony began inside the church hall with prayers, and an usher came to give them copies of the program.

Lola's father opened her side door and asked, "Are you ready?"

"Yes." Lola was definitely ready for this long-awaited moment. She had been ready for some time. She had even practiced how to walk down the aisle at a dignified pace. She had seen some brides walk down the aisle too fast.

Her white wedding gown, veil, and accessories had been carefully chosen, and she looked absolutely beautiful. Her hair had also been well styled, and she felt very beautiful. *This is the day that the Lord has made, and I will rejoice and be glad in it,* she told herself.

When she got down from the car, her father offered her his arm and she took it.

As they made their way to the door of the hall, she remembered that she was supposed to hold her bouquet low, so people could see the front of her wedding dress well, and she lowered the flower. The beautiful ball gown with a sweetheart neckline and sweeping train had bead embellishments and lace applique.

The bridal train had lined up at the main door of the sanctuary and when the processional hymn began, they began to go in.

Soon, Lola, on her father's arm, was walking down the aisle with joy, also singing the hymn: *Great is Thy faithfulness*. The best lady was behind Lola, carrying out her duty, while Sarah followed the best lady, happy for her friend, Lola.

People turned to look at Lola and her father as they gracefully made their way down the aisle to the altar. The hall had been transformed with drapes and balloons of different colors for the occasion.

In front, Lola's father released her hand and as she took her place beside John, all eyes were on her, including John's who looked very handsome in his well-tailored black suit. He liked what he saw—Lola's gown did not expose her body unnecessarily, yet she looked both elegant and graceful, he thought and smiled at his bride. She was also smiling and her face glowed.

Her father went to stand beside his wife while the best lady stood by her seat behind the bride. Sarah went to join her husband.

Glancing around, Lola saw the officiating ministers, the choir, and John's parents who wore the same cream-colored attire, where they sat. She also noticed that her father was beside his wife, a couple was next to them, and then Seun Alabi, Grandpa, and Grandma.

The ceremony progressed and when it was time for the solemnization, the senior pastor of the church came to stand on the altar, and asked Lola and John to stand.

Then he began, "Dearly beloved, we are gathered here in the sight of God and in the presence of these witnesses, to join together this man and this woman in holy matrimony, which is an honorable estate, instituted by God. It is therefore not to be entered into unadvisedly, but reverently, discreetly, and in the fear of God."

The service continued and soon, Lola and John faced each other and taking turns, said “I do". They exchanged their wedding vows and rings which the pastor had blessed, and the pastor prayed for them.

The pastor continued, “As John and Lola have given themselves to each other by the promises they have exchanged, I now pronounce them husband and wife, in the name of the Father, and of the Son, and of the Holy Spirit.”

The congregation said *Amen*.

He went on. “Let everyone everywhere recognize and respect this holy union now and forever.”

The congregation said *Amen* again.

“You may now kiss your bride.” The pastor told John.

Amidst cheers, he turned to Lola for their very first kiss.

Afterward, the pastor asked them to face the congregation, and holding hands, John and Lola turned.

“I introduce to you for the first time, Mr. and Mrs.—”

This introduction elicited cheers and applause from families, friends, and well-wishers who had shown up to witness their union.

The pastor finished introducing them and beaming, the new couple waved their second hands at the people. Suddenly, Lola spotted Lekan and Victor, they were seated by the aisle that she and John would pass when the service ended. Mercy was beside Lekan, and on Mercy’s left side were Stella and her husband.

When she told John, he looked in the direction, and waved at them.

Lola and John returned to their seats, and as the choristers who wore purple and yellow robes filed out to the front to render two special songs, Lola told John, “I’m still amazed, dazed in fact, by what God has done and how He did it—Lekan and Victor, you and me! Indeed, God rules in the affairs of men."

He agreed. "No matter what we plan, God has a bigger and better plan."

"Wow!"

After the choir ministration, John's pastor, Dave, gave a brief exhortation in which he admonished married couples never to leave God out of their affairs. At the end, he made altar call, and some of the people who came out to give their lives to Jesus were movie stars. Afterward, he prayed for the new couple while they knelt.

About twenty minutes after, the lovely ceremony was brought to a close with the recessional hymn: *Guide me O, Thou great Jehovah.* A grand reception would follow in an event center not too far from the church.

As the new couple exited the hall hand in hand, followed by their best man and best lady, photographers snapped away.

John and Lola looked and smiled at the many guests present to celebrate their love, including movie stars and movie producers.

When they got to where Lekan and the others were standing, they waved at them, and the five people waved back.

Some people would claim that the get-together in January was fortuitous for them, accidentally bringing them together, but being Christians, Lola and John knew that it was no accident. God did it, working behind the scenes.

ALSO BY TAIWO IREDELE ODUBIYI

FICTION

Pratt Sisters Series
In Love for Us * Tears on My Pillow * To Love Again

Femi and Ibie Series
With This Ring * The Forever Kind of Love

Agape Campus Church Series
You Found Me * Life Goes On * My Desire

Bible Stories
What Changed You? * Too Much of a Good Thing

The Past Series
Shadows from the Past * This Time Around * Then Came You

Baby Miracle Series
Oh Baby! * Sea of Regrets

Redirected Series
Is it Me You're Looking for? * Marriage on Fire * Shipwrecked With You

Mercy & friends Series
The Forever Kind of Love * If You Could See Me Now

Stand Alone Titles

Love Fever * Love on the Pulpit * My First Love
* The One for Me
* When A Man Loves A Woman * I'll Take You There
* Never Say Never!

FOR CHILDREN

Rescued by Victor * No One is a Nobody
* Greater Tomorrow * The Boy Who Stole
* Joe and His Stepmother, Bibi * Nike & the Stranger
* Billy the Bully * Jonah's First Day of School

NONFICTION

30 Things Husbands Do That Hurt Their Wives
* 30 Things Wives Do That Hurt Their Husbands
* Rape & How to Handle it * Devotionals for Singles
* God's Words to Singles * God's Words to Couples
* God's Words to Older Adults
* Real Answers, Real Quick! (for singles)
* Real Answers, Real Quick! (for couples)
* Divine Instructions to live by – 1
* Divine Instructions to live by – 2
* God's Words to Women in Ministry

ABOUT THE AUTHOR

Taiwo Iredele Odubiyi is a Pastor and the Executive President of TenderHearts Family Support Initiative, a Non-Governmental Organization, and Pastor Taiwo Odubiyi Ministries. She has a deep and strong passion for relationships and expresses this in ministries - nationally and internationally- to children, teenagers, singles, women and couples. She reaches out to these groups through counselling, seminars and programs such as Teenslink, Singleslink, Coupleslink, and Woman to Woman.

Married and blessed with children, she is the regular host of the TV and Radio program—It's all about you!

This is the twenty eighth of her soul-lifting and life-changing novels.

I love hearing from the readers of my books. If this book has blessed you, please send your comments to:

WhatsApp: +1(443)694-6228
Website: www.pastortaiwoodubiyi.org
Facebook: Pastor Mrs. Taiwo Odubiyi
Pastor Taiwo Iredele Odubiyi's novels & books
Twitter: @pastortaiwoodub
Instagram: @pastortaiwoiredeleodubiyi

If you have friends and loved ones, then you do have people you should bless with copies of these very interesting and life-changing novels and books!

Printed in Great Britain
by Amazon

26338092R00108